*11-09*

## THE HAIR STOOD UP
## ON THE BACK OF MATT'S NECK

Two missing men . . . and now someone—a wraith-like figure moving silently and quickly through the undergrowth—was following the priest.

Suddenly, the adrenaline boiled through Matt's veins. Although he had never seen an Apache, Matt knew that the lone figure crouched across the gully was an Apache warrior. Matt knew he was looking at the real thing.

# RAMSEY'S REVENGE

## WILL McLENNAN

JOVE BOOKS, NEW YORK

RAMSEY'S REVENGE

A Jove Book / published by arrangement with
the author

PRINTING HISTORY
Jove edition / October 1991

ISBN: 0-515-10707-7

Jove Books are published by The Berkley Publishing Group,
200 Madison Avenue, New York, New York 10016.
The name "JOVE" and the "J" logo
are trademarks belonging to Jove Publications, Inc.

PRINTED IN THE UNITED STATES OF AMERICA

10 9 8 7 6 5 4 3 2 1

# CHAPTER
# ★ 1 ★

The buckskin stopped at the crest of the little wartlike hill. The pack burro, carrying two large wooden casks of water, halted, too, its nose close to the flank of the horse. Matt Ramsey, his eyes red-rimmed from staring into the unrelenting sun of southwestern Arizona Territory, turned slowly in the saddle . . . first to the right . . . then to the left. Finally he glanced back over his shoulder. Nothing had changed. It was the same harsh and tedious landscape that he had been viewing through heat waves for the better part of three days.

He was glad he had taken the advice of the rivermen back in the ramshackle community of Ehrenberg on the banks of the wide-running Colorado River. Glad that he had brought the water-bearing burro. When they said there was no water between the river and Phoenix, they had told him true. Not even a seeping spring, they had said. Not even a catchment in a rocky canyon arroyo.

The distance from the river to Phoenix was a hundred and fifty miles . . . and from his reckoning, Matt Ramsey figured he had forty or fifty miles left. Tough trip, no doubt about it. He shook his head and wondered at the wisdom of his decision. You must want to see old Cleve awful bad, he told himself. Then he smiled. His desire to see Cleve was only part of it. Actually, he admitted to himself, he didn't

1

really have much of anyplace else to go.

Matt removed a canvas water bag from the saddle horn and took a drink of the water. It was nearly hot enough to make coffee with, he conjectured. After he had capped the water bag, he sat for a while, studying the terrain ahead. The heat made travel almost unbearable, but the real problem was the mountains. On all sides they rose out of the undulating flatland of the Arizona desert. Jagged, ugly mountains, with steep boulder-strewn sides and nearly impassable canyons.

The best way . . . the easiest way, of course . . . was to go around the mountains. So far, he had. But now Matt was in a situation where "going around" would mean, maybe, an extra thirty or forty miles. At least, that was the way it looked. And then, if he got boxed in again . . . possibly thirty or forty more. He raised his dark eyebrows and sighed. Off there, to the southeast, it seemed that there might be a fairly negotiable pass between a pair of ragged peaks. He decided to give it a try.

Matt jiggled the reins, and the buckskin moved forward through the greasewood and spiny cholla, the uncomplaining burro following at the end of its rawhide tether.

Matt was tiring of the never-changing view . . . the starkly pale, sun-drenched sky . . . the rumpled sawtooth mountains on every side. But more than anything else, Matt Ramsey was tired and beaten down by the bloody heat. As hot, he told himself, as the breath from some demon blast furnace. He hoped that Cleve Madison's ranch down near the Mexican border was in more hospitable country. The letter he had received from Cleve almost two years ago had said the country was nice . . . "nearly stirrup-deep in grass . . . in the shadow of some mighty big mountains." If that's so, Matt told himself, I suppose I can stand another few days of hell's heat.

As Matt rode toward the distant pass . . . or what he hoped was a pass . . . he couldn't help but reflect on the circuitous and profitless route that was taking him to a reunion with his old Civil War friend.

It had all started when he and Bucky made a trip up to Colorado, hoping to straighten out the bitter, hard-drinking lifestyle of brother Kyle. They definitely hadn't wrought any major changes in the way Kyle handled his affairs, but something *had* changed Matt. Gold fever. At some point in time, up in Colorado, the ordinarily sensible Matt Ramsey had contracted an acute case of gold fever. As he rode, Matt couldn't help but allow a bemused smile to form. How, he wondered, could he have fallen for the siren song of the goldfields? But he had.

For a considerable period of time after he and young Bucky had parted company, Matt had rattled around in the area of Gregory Gulch, not far from the place where brother Kyle was washing dirt. During that period of time, Matt observed that the most promising strikes had been bought up by big mining interests. Eventually most of the local prospectors wound up working for the big companies . . . receiving near-starvation wages for dangerous and backbreaking work. And that was the end of the dream for most of them.

Matt, tiring of Colorado, and believing—as all victims of gold fever do—that the digging and panning would be better over the next hill, drifted west across Utah and into Nevada. There he wandered from Tonopah to Goldfield . . . then on north to Rawhide. In Nevada, as elsewhere, the rich mines all belonged to big companies. And for every prospector who found a nugget, there were a thousand who did not. As one old prospector told Matt, "Seems every place I go, I either arrive too late or leave too soon." It seemed to Matt that the same thing was happening to him. One day the message came to him as clear as a bolt from the blue. "Time to get out," the message said. So Matt Ramsey hearkened to the message and, that very day he left.

At first he simply rode east, back in the general and nonspecific direction of his old home state of Texas. But less than a hundred miles out of Rawhide, he started thinking about Cleve and his big spread down in the southernmost part of untamed Arizona Territory. It was as simple as flicking the reins and aiming his mount in a southerly direction. That was how Matt Ramsey had been making decisions for a long time.

Ever since the end of the War Between the States, ever since he had been paroled at Vicksburg and come back West to a Texas that had changed so much he couldn't really stay there anymore, Matt Ramsey had been looking for something to sink his teeth into . . . something that would get him settled back into a way of life that might produce rewards that were tangible and permanent. Good-paying work . . . maybe some land of his own . . . maybe even a wife and family. But none of that had happened, and Matt Ramsey sometimes wondered if he was destined to wander always. He didn't have the answer to that ponderable question, and with the desert heat inflaming his nostrils and burning his brow, he really wasn't in the mood for serious thinking. Getting to Phoenix before his water ran out was really the matter of topmost priority.

The mountain Matt was aiming toward was still a good three miles away. It would be midafternoon by the time he got there. It would be a hot, slow three miles . . . like all the other miles between him and the river. Coming down the river had actually been the best part of the trip. It was near Fort Mohave on the eastern edge of Nevada, just below the point where the Colorado came boiling out of the Grand Canyon, that Matt had bought passage south on one of the river steamers. Being on the water . . . being near the water . . . made it tolerable. But the desert was a different matter. Matt was longing for nightfall and the sudden, soothing drop in heat that always came in the desert with the disappearing sun.

When the buckskin came to a deep and sandy arroyo, Matt let the horse angle down to the dry streambed. The smooth, hard-packed sand was easier on the horse and easier on Matt. There were no needle-sharp cacti growing in the arroyo. Matt had already experienced the invasion of sharp cholla spines twice on the trip, and the opportunity to ride without constantly watching for cactus plants was a measurable blessing. Besides, from Matt's appraisal, it appeared that the snaky path of the arroyo was angling in the desired direction.

Matt might have dozed in the saddle and let the horse follow the arroyo on its own, but the heat was a deterrent to that. Instead, Matt occupied himself by reflecting on the last time he had seen Cleve Madison. Strange, thought Matt, but I can't even recall how many years ago that was. Six . . . maybe seven years back.

That last time had been at Cleve's wedding. During the war years, when they marched and fought together for the Confederate side, Cleve had often spoken of his love for Alicia Graves. And, somehow, Matt had created a mental picture of a lovely, spirited Texas beauty, for that was the way Cleve made it sound when he spoke of her . . . and he spoke often. When, finally, with the war over, Matt made her acquaintance at the wedding in a little church in Nacogdoches, Texas, he felt for the first few moments that something strange had happened . . . that a new bride had been run in for the sweet and supple Alicia he had fashioned in his mind. But no. The bride was the real Alicia. Maybe the best way to put it was that Matt was truly glad . . . glad all the way down to his boot tips that Alicia was going to Cleve and not to him.

First of all—to Matt at least—Cleve's Alicia seemed entirely devoid of personality. During the entire day that Matt was around the woman, he never noticed the slightest change in her facial expression. Alicia Graves hadn't even smiled when Cleve slipped the ring on her finger . . . hadn't smiled when the guests were offering toasts to their perpetual happiness and well-being. And she surely hadn't smiled when Matt Ramsey attempted to entertain her with his conversation. No, she hadn't given him even a twitch of a smile, although she well knew that he was among her husband's best and closest friends.

On top of all that, Alicia's listless personality was matched by an equally unimpressive physical appearance. That's the way she appeared to Matt. It wasn't that her features were poor . . . they weren't. But her color, in Matt's eyes, matched the eternal dullness of her mannerisms. Her hair, pulled back severely, was straw-colored. Her skin, without the slightest blush at the cheeks, without discernible color at the lips, was a pasty, uniform white. On top of that, her eyes . . . the palest blue . . . looked washed-out, too.

On the other hand, Alicia Graves presented a more than ample and well-proportioned bosom. In fact, as the day wore on, Matt found himself looking more at Alicia's bosom than at her face. But his final conclusion was that it would take a very long and very cold winter night before the allure of her breasts might conceivably overcome the deficit of her personality and blank expression.

So Matt's unannounced visit to Cleve Madison, owner of some two thousand acres of southern Arizona cattle land, offered apparently mixed opportunities. True enough, he was eager to spend some time with his old Civil War friend, but engaging on a personal basis with listless Alicia was not a particularly enticing proposition.

Matt wondered, too, how Cleve was doing in the tough frontier climate of territorial Arizona. He knew that the area where Cleve was ranching had belonged to Mexico until the Gadsden Purchase of 1853. According to news reports and word-of-mouth tales, southern Arizona wasn't an easy place to live . . . not even an easy place to survive. More than anything else, the fierce and wide-ranging Apache made it so. Supposedly, the Apache had been brought under a measure of control since the end of the war, but the rivermen back in Ehrenberg had told Matt to keep an eye out. Even though the majority of the Apache were now confined to the reservation at San Carlos, located in the east central part of the territory, a few of the desert marauders were still on the loose, raiding stock and killing settlers.

Up ahead the streambed widened. On the south side a tangled growth of mesquite trees grew to the very edge of the wash, branches hanging over the bank, casting shade down on the sandy bottom. Good place to stop and give the animals a drink, Matt told himself.

He halted the horse and dismounted in the relative coolness of the shadows cast by the trees on the high bank above. Matt removed a wooden pail from the pack saddle on the burro, then filled it half-full with water from one of the casks. Then, he moved around the burro and walked between the horse and the near-vertical, ten-foot embankment.

The sudden, harsh buzz propelled him back from the dirt wall. The horse shied at the same moment, causing a momentary, water-sloshing encounter between man and steed. The rattler was on a narrow ledge about five feet above the streambed. Dozing, no doubt, in the shade, Matt told himself . . . until he had arrived to disturb it.

Matt grabbed the reins and calmed the buckskin . . . then walked both the horse and burro a few paces down the wash. He pulled his Winchester .44 out of the saddle holster and eased back toward the place where the rattler was lying. No longer coiled, the five-foot, wrist-thick snake was sliding easily along the ledge, heading for a point where a tangle of exposed mesquite roots emerged from the hard-packed bank. Matt stood, eight feet away, and watched it.

He was about to throw a cartridge into the chamber, but he hesitated . . . intrigued by the smooth gliding progress of the venomous snake. Hell, he told himself, there's not a child, a farm dog, a domesticated animal, except for mine, within a hundred miles of this place. Why kill it? he asked himself. This is his land, not mine.

Matt stooped and picked up a handful of sand, tossed it at the rattler. Instantly the big snake wrapped itself into a tight coil, aimed its dangerous-looking head in Matt's direction, and buzzed furiously. Now Matt spoke aloud. "I hear your warnin', friend. I'm leavin'. You can have this place." Then he turned and walked away.

# CHAPTER
★ 2 ★

The foothills of the gray and ragged mountains were more distant than Matt had estimated. The sun was close to the western horizon by the time he and his animals started up the lower slopes. Rough country, and the way would get rougher if the pass didn't materialize. But he thought it would. The deep canyon between the peaks was even more distinct than it had been from a distance.

Once into the canyon the buckskin's line of travel intersected with a very distinct animal trail. After moving along the trail for nearly a mile, Matt heard a clattering in the rocks ahead, then caught sight of the desert bighorns . . . a dozen or more of them . . . clambering up the steep sides of the canyon, racing away from his intrusion. So that's it, he told himself; that's what made the trail. He halted the horse and watched as now they bounded gracefully along the lip of a nearly sheer, hundred-foot cliff. He found it hard to believe that animals so large could survive in the parched confines of the desert. But, apparently, they could, and he admired them for it.

By the time the sun had started behind the hills to the west, Matt was satisfied that his route would, indeed, take him out of the mountains on the eastern side. Unless darkness caught him, he would continue on until he made it back to the flatlands, where he could lay his roll on soft sand rather than the sharp rocks of the canyon.

Shortly the walls closed in on either side . . . barren cliffs that rose dramatically upward, confining Matt, horse, and burro into a defile less than ten feet wide. At a sharp turn in the path the horse shied, snorted, and danced uncertainly on the loose rock surface.

When the animal finally settled down, Matt sat quietly . . . listening. No sounds came to his ears; nevertheless, he slipped the rifle from its scabbard. Then he urged his mount forward. As soon as the horse negotiated the turn, the source of the buckskin's fright became abundantly and shockingly apparent.

The man was hanging upside down, suspended by rawhide thongs from a protruding boulder about nine feet above the trail. Actually, it was not a man. It was the remains of man.

Matt studied it with a deep measure of solemnity. And with fear as well. He could feel the surge of adrenaline that set his defensive faculties in motion. The hairs stood up on the back of his neck. The horse didn't like it, either. It snorted and danced some more.

Matt's eyes narrowed as he studied the corpse. Surely it must have been hanging there for a long time . . . months perhaps. Matt could tell by the color of the sunbaked flesh that the man had been skinned . . . probably while he was hanging there. That, Matt told himself, was a deed that could have been done only by Apache. The man—or what was left of the man—was as stiff as dried jerky. About the same color, too.

The corpse had no head. That wasn't too hard for Matt to figure out, either. On the ground, and up against the cliff, were a number of charred hunks of wood and a scattering of old charcoal. Matt had heard the grisly stories many times. They hung the victim upside down, skinned him alive . . . then built a fire under the head and cooked it until it exploded.

If the hanging corpse was a warning to white intruders, it was having the desired effect. Slowly, and as quietly as he could, Matt worked the lever on the Winchester and slid a cartridge into the chamber . . . just in case. Actually, however, the analytical part of his mind was telling him that there was, most likely, no present danger. The dead man had been there a long time. Those who had put him there were months gone . . . surely. On the other hand . . . maybe not.

What to do with the remains? Matt wanted out of the canyon. He had absolutely no desire to tarry any longer than necessary. Yet he felt an obligation to do *something* about the corpse. He thought about it. If there were Apache nearby and he started digging, their keen ears would easily pick up the sound of shovel against rocks.

He thought about it some more. If he did take the poor devil down and laid him in a shallow grave, the coyotes would undoubtedly unearth the remains and scatter the bones after they had finished gnawing on them. In the heat and hard rock there was no way he could dig a hole deep enough to give the dead man a proper burial.

Finally Matt made his decision. He pressed his heels against the horse and flicked the reins. As he passed by, Matt removed his hat and whispered softly, "God, please accept this poor man's soul."

That night Matt camped without making a fire . . . ate some dried biscuits and chewed on a few strips of jerky. Truth to tell, it was more than a little difficult to get the sun-dried beef down his throat. It looked too much like the dead man's flesh.

Under a brilliant canopy of stars Matt sat on his blanket and wondered why Cleve Madison had ever decided to leave the lush pine forests of east Texas for the wilds of Arizona. On the other hand, it really wasn't all that difficult to figure out. Cleve Madison was a man who loved adventure. Things over in east Texas were just too settled and soft for a man like Cleve, whose father had died while he was gone to war, leaving him three large sawmills and some impressive stands of good timber. No doubt about it, Cleve could have chosen the soft and easy life, lived out his days in comfort on what his daddy had willed him. But Cleve wasn't that kind of man. So he sold it all, then took the money, along with bland Alicia, and headed for Arizona, where he bought up land in a place called the Altar Valley on the eastern side of some high desert mountains known as the Baboquivari. "If you want to visit or want a job, just come on out," Cleve had written in the old and only letter Matt had ever received from him. Well . . . now he was on his way . . . if the Apache or something else didn't get him before he got there.

Out in the brush a desert owl hooted twice. Then, from a more distant point off to the left, another owl responded with just one hoot. Matt was sure that the hoots had come from real owls . . . but he wasn't absolutely sure . . . not sure beyond a shadow of a doubt. And, for that measure of doubt, Matt stayed awake for a long time.

While he sat there in the dark, Matt wondered how the Apache could treat another human being as cruelly as they had treated the dead man in the canyon. Yet, Matt was privy to what the tidal wave of white men had done to the Indians in Texas, all throughout the Midwest, for that matter. Matt believed that there was enough land for all . . . believed that men should learn to live together. But experience had taught him that fear and greed, along with other human defects, were a great impediment to social harmony. Lots of people wanted to deny that the land had first belonged to the Indian. Lots of people, to ease the burden of their deeds, even took the position that Indians weren't really on the same evolutionary level as whites.

So . . . they took the land, made hollow promises, and killed the Indians when the natives evidenced that they didn't like what was happening to their ancient culture and their ancestral lands.

The Apache, Matt had been told, were more immune to the lies and hollow promises of the whites than any other Indians on the continent. And they were also some of the toughest, most fearsome fighters that had ever gone out to war. Bad times make men do bad things. Matt Ramsey knew how that worked. Still, he felt real sorry for the unfortunate wretch he had found hanging in the canyon. Matt had witnessed a lot of unpleasant things in his time, but the headless man hung by his ankles was, without doubt, the most brutal sight he had ever seen.

Sometime toward midnight the owls stopped hooting. Finally Matt, exhausted and with the Winchester at his side, fell into an uncomfortable and dream-disturbed sleep.

# CHAPTER

## ★ 3 ★

Phoenix was a scattering of rude buildings, mostly low adobe structures with roofs composed of wattles covered with sun-dried mud. And, like all of the hundred and fifty miles that Matt Ramsey had crossed on his trek east from the Colorado River, Phoenix was hot.

Matt laid over in the desert community for a day, giving the horse and burro a chance to rest in the shade of a livery stable stall. Matt took a room in a recommended hotel. The man-on-the-street who did the recommending said it was the only place in town cool enough to sleep during the day. Well, Matt told himself as he tossed uncomfortably on a lumpy surface that soon became damp from his perspiration, it was almost tolerable . . . but not quite. However, the man-on-the-street had been partly right. The heavy adobe walls, nearly three feet thick, did, indeed, provide a partial barrier against the blistering heat.

Matt's real impediment to daytime sleep was the parade of scorpions that marched up and down the walls of the room. They were little brown desert scorpions that could temporarily paralyze a human limb with the stab of a venomous tail. When Matt rented the room in the single-story building, the hotel manager had acknowledged their presence. "Ain't nothin' that will truly get rid of 'em. God knows, we've tried," the man told Matt. "As long as they

13

don't get in your bed, you'll be all right." The man also pointed out how each leg of the bed stood in a small container of kerosene. "They don't swim," he said reassuringly as he made his exit.

Matt, with a leery eye, watched the scorpions for a while . . . then exhaustion called and he dozed off. But sleep lasted for less than an hour. True, the temperature inside the room was fifteen to eighteen degrees cooler than outside, but with the exterior heat near a hundred and twenty, the room wasn't exactly an ice cave.

So Matt, after awakening, laid on his back with his arms folded behind his head and watched the scorpion parade. They moved slowly, maybe four or five visible at any one time, meandering toward no place in particular. Maybe just lookin' for someone to stab, Matt conjectured.

Finally he let his gaze move from walls to ceiling, and that was when Matt decided to get up, get dressed, and tour the town. One of the scorpions going up the wall had taken a hard right at the point where wall and ceiling joined and was walking, upside down, across the ceiling on a path that would soon put him directly over the bed.

In the Rising Bird Saloon a one-eyed patron told Matt that there was a visible wagon trail between Phoenix and Tucson. "From Tucson to Tubac . . . how far is that?" Matt inquired.

"About fifty miles," the one-eyed man replied. "But what takes you down there? The Apache run everybody off some years back. Tubac's deserted."

"I thought all the Apache had been put on a reservation," Matt replied.

"True . . . true," the man told him. "But the main problem, you see, is that there ain't no fence around that reservation. As a matter of fact, it covers over two thousand square miles. Ain't no way for the troops—and there ain't many of 'em—to keep track of every Indian. So they leave if they want to . . . whenever they feel like it."

"Is a man likely to run across a bunch . . . out raidin', I mean?"

The man studied his warm beer for a moment and decided to be rigorously honest with the newcomer. "Truth to tell, I guess it's not much more dangerous out on the land these days than it is right in this saloon on a Saturday night. Maybe safer, to tell the truth. But it's best to keep an eye out. The problem down around Tubac ain't that the Apache are raidin' so much anymore. It's just that after the people was run off by the Apache, durin' the war years, the settlers never came back. It's lonely country down that way."

Later on Matt found a general store and stocked up on supplies. In the midafternoon he treated himself to a professional shave in an adobe barbershop with a dirt floor. And then, when the sun went down, he bought a home-cooked meal in a boardinghouse . . . walked the streets for a while . . . and after the temperature dipped below ninety-five, he went back to his hotel room. Matt Ramsey was bone tired from his journey across western Arizona . . . so tired, in fact, that he didn't bother to light the lantern or even to check on his sharp-tailed, wall-crawling roommates. He merely removed his clothes, fell on the bed, and lapsed into deep sleep.

Two days later Matt passed through the gates of the walled city of Tucson. Tucson was in higher, more tolerable country. The monotonous flatness of the central section of the territory had given way to rolling hills, thick desert growth, and tall, stately saguaros that extended their uplifted arms toward a sky of purest blue. Nearly fifteen hundred feet higher in altitude and with daytime temperatures just a tad over a hundred degrees, Tucson was far more comfortable than the central desert.

"It's even cooler down in the country to the south," a Mexican merchant told Matt. "Good land . . . but no people."

"I'm going down to a ranch . . . place owned by a friend of mine . . . called the Circle M."

The Mexican man pursed his lips and thought a bit. "I have not heard of it."

"In the Altar Valley."

Now the man wrinkled his forehead . . . thought some more. "No, I never heard of that place, either."

"West of Tubac."

"Ah," said the Mexican man, "I know where Tubac is . . . near the old mission of Tumacacori. But, as I said, very few people down there."

The one-eyed man in Phoenix and the Mexican merchant in Tucson had been right about the absence of people. Matt passed the last discernible sign of habitation about five miles south of the walled city. After that he saw no one. Nevertheless, the ride south was, without doubt, the best part of Matt's journey through Arizona Territory. As suggested by the people in Tucson, he followed the nearly dry streambed of the Santa Cruz River. "It'll take you right into Tubac," he had been told. Even though the river was only a foot-wide trickle in a streambed that was over a hundred feet across, trees grew along the banks . . . mostly desert mesquite and hardy cottonwoods.

Off to Matt's left . . . to the east . . . rose the stately and impressive Santa Rita Mountains, and from time to time, when Matt was riding over an elevated rise, he could see vast sweeps of grassland in the distance. Quail called from out in the brush, and floppy-eared jackrabbits bounded frequently across his path. Already Matt was liking the land that Cleve Madison had chosen for his new home.

In early afternoon of the second day out of Tucson, Matt arrived at the presidio of Tubac. Once Arizona's largest community of people, the stillness and the quiet told Matt that the information given to him in Phoenix and Tucson had been correct. No dogs barked . . . no roosters crowed. Only silence. Yet, he had been told in Tucson that a man named Riggs maintained the semblance of a store in Tubac, a place that sometimes served the ranchers, wandering prospectors, and travelers passing through. "Riggs is a tough old man," he was told. "He stayed down there all through the years of the Apache rampage. Holed up in a thick-walled section of the presidio. The Indians couldn't run him off, and tales have it he killed dozens of 'em durin' that period."

Now, looking for Riggs and his store, Matt rode slowly through the deserted streets of Tubac. He passed one empty building after another . . . all with shutterless windows and gaping doorways. Weeds grew deep in Tubac's plaza. At the southernmost area of the abandoned community, Matt noticed a rock structure that stood behind a thick, plastered wall. Garments were hanging on a clothesline, flapping in the desert wind, and green vines—recently watered by someone—were climbing up the wall. But it was the crude, weathered sign above the plank gate that told Matt, without doubt, that he had arrived at Riggs's store. That's because the sign said, "Riggs's Store."

Matt dismounted and tied the horse to a post. There was another sign . . . smaller and with a hand-scrawled message beside the heavy gate. Matt squinted to read it. It said:

There is so dam many bad people ayround, you beder
ring the bell befor cumin in els I will shoot you.

Matt rang the bell. It was a large bell, not the tinkly, little kind found on hardware store counters. It bonged loud enough, Matt thought, to wake a dead man at a hundred paces. Matt removed his stained hat, ran his fingers through his dark hair, and waited. He had no intention whatsoever of going through the gate until invited. Not with Riggs, the slayer of many Apache, on the other side.

After a considerable period a hollow voice boomed out from the other side of the gate. "Who is it and what do you want?"

"Name's Matt Ramsey. I'm passin' through on my way to the Circle M Ranch. I need some directions and a little grub."

Again the hollow voice boomed out. "Any weapons on your body needs to be off and held above your head. Once you done that, you can open the gate and come through."

Matt unbuckled his gunbelt, held the holstered Colt above his head, flipped the iron latch, and entered the yard.

"Stop."

Matt stopped and waited, shifting his eyes from left to right and back again, looking for the source of the voice. He figured that Riggs was behind one of the heavily shuttered windows . . . probably peeking out of an aperture or a crack in the boards.

"Turn a little left."

Matt turned a little left.

"Well, you ain't no Mexican bandit. I can see that. There's a wooden box beside the path. Put your weapon in there. Then lock the box with that lock hangin' on the hasp."

Matt walked to the heavy wooden box that was sitting four feet off the ground on a solid wooden post. He did as the voice instructed.

As soon as the box was locked, the front door of the building opened, and a grizzled, unshaven man on the far side of fifty stepped out. The barrel of the shotgun was aimed only casually in Matt's direction. Now the voice was cheery. "Come on in. Sorry for the inconvenience, but I got to be careful with strangers."

The interior of the place featured shelves on the walls and a loose assortment of tables that held merchandise of one type or another. In an open space several wooden chairs were arranged around a large upturned crate that obviously served as a table. "Sit," said the man. "My name's Riggs."

"Assumed it was," Matt said with a slight smile.

"Coffee, whiskey, or cool water . . . the first drink's always on me."

Matt thought about it for a moment. "I think I'll try the coffee."

Riggs joined him with a hot coffeepot and two mugs. "Headin' for the Circle M, eh?"

"That, I am," Matt replied. "And I'm travelin' on the basis of a letter I received some two years ago. From an old friend. An invitation to visit. The letter said his ranch is about twenty-five miles west of Tubac. I thought maybe you could give me some directions on how to get out there."

Riggs poured for both of them, then settled back. "Well," the old man said, "the letter told about all you need to know. Twenty-five miles west of here. That's where it is." He took a sip of coffee. "There's a high mountain peak straight west from here, called Baboquivari Peak . . . the highest point in the Baboquivari Mountains. You leave here . . . aim for that peak and you can't miss it. The main house, corrals, and barns are on the far side of the valley at the base of the foothills."

Matt sat in the cool interior of Riggs's store for a considerable period of time, resting, drinking the old man's coffee, and picking up a lot of local history and information. Matt was most intrigued by Riggs's story of his long-running battle with the Apache.

"Me, my wife, and boy lived out aways from the town proper. Had a pretty nice spread out there to the east, on the far side of the Santa Cruz. Raised some cattle . . . had some crops. We had a Mexican lady that did the cookin' and a few Mexican hands to help out. Every once in a while the Apache would steal a few horses. We shot at them a little, and they shot back from time to time. But all that changed when the War Between the States got fired up. The Apache went plumb wild."

"How come?" Matt asked. "What made 'em go so wild?"

"Troops left to go to the war. When that happened, the Apache leaders congratulated their warriors and told them that they had driven all of the white soldiers off the land."

A large black cat slid silently across the room and leaped effortlessly into Riggs's lap, where it immediately closed its eyes and went to sleep. "So," Matt said, "with the troops gone, the Apache believed they could raid wherever and whenever they wanted to."

"And they did," Riggs replied. "They hit us two, three times a month. Got two of my cowboys out on the range over east near the Santa Ritas. Attacked us here so many times I lost count. But we held 'em off pretty good. Me and the hands fortified the main house. Boarded up all the windows, knocked gunports in the walls, and built a rock wall all around the place. Want more coffee?"

Matt nodded that he did, and Riggs dumped the cat on the floor and disappeared into the next room, returning shortly with the coffeepot and a plate of cold tamales wrapped in corn husks. "Ever eat a cold tamale?" the old man asked. Matt shook his head in the negative. "Hot tamales cold. That's what I call 'em."

"Actually," Matt told him, "I've never eaten a tamale either way."

"Well, in that case, you better try one. Now, these, even though they're cold . . . they're hot. Lots of pepper dust in these babies. I like 'em that way. Good for your gut, too. Ain't never heard of a Mexican yet with stomach trouble." The old man helped himself to one of the tamales and peeled off the dried husks. "Open 'em up like this."

Matt followed suit and soon was savoring the hot yet appealing flavor of his first tamale.

Old Riggs continued his story. "One day about five years back, my boy . . . he was a little past nine years then . . . was out by the corral, playin' in a pile of hay. It was a nice cool fall day, bright and cloudless. Well, I guess he got some tuckered, so he climbed up on the hay and dozed off. Ramon—one of my hands—seen it from up on the hill. Six Apache rode out of the big arroyo and grabbed Jimmy even before he was awake. Threw him on the ground, and one of them devils pushed an eight-foot war lance right through him. Ramon started shootin', and they shot back. Ramon had to duck for cover. I was two or three miles out on the range. Heard the shootin' and started back in. By the time I got here, the Apache had made off with all the horses in the corral. Jimmy was dead."

"I'm sorry to hear that," Matt said.

Riggs went on. "Little over a year later they got my wife. She was in a wagon, comin' out from the presidio here at Tubac. I told her never to do that, but she was a strong-willed, fearless woman." It seemed to Matt that Riggs's eyes got watery as he spoke of his wife. He sniffed rather loudly. "Don't know how many they wuz. But when we found her, there was lots of empty cartridge shells in the wagon. She give 'em a hell of a fight . . . killed one of 'em.

We found him in some bushes 'bout fifty yards from where she died. They took the horses. That was all they wanted. Killed her for the horses." Riggs sniffed again.

Matt repeated his earlier sentiment. "I'm real, real sorry to hear that."

"I sent all the help off. By that time everyone had left Tubac anyway. So, bein' Mexicans, they went south across the border to Magdalena, I s'pose. That left only me. Couldn't work the place anymore, so I come into the presidio. Found me a part of the fort that could be easily barricaded. I just hung on. That's all. I rode out a lot . . . lookin' for them devils that killed my wife. I guess they thought I was crazy . . . or maybe possessed by some kind of demon. But it finally got so that when they saw me comin'—even if there was ten or twelve of 'em—they'd run like hell. I used to lie in hidin'. I ambushed quite a few of 'em that way. A few times I guess they decided to get rid of me. So they'd put together a war party of twenty or thirty and come into Tubac lookin' for me. That's the way it was . . . sometimes they ran from me . . . sometimes they come after me. Guess I've killed me more than forty Apache. But I finally decided I'd never kill enough to wipe out my sorrow. So I eased off. Then the war was over and soon the troops come back. I decided to open me a store . . . this here store you're sittin' in right now." He smiled and took a long drink of coffee. "But the people are slow comin' back. Sometimes I think that maybe they won't ever come back."

"I think they'll be back," Matt told him. "I've been through a lot of country in the past few years, and the people are still comin' . . . still movin' west."

"It's lonely out here, so I do enjoy a visitor like yourself. Pete Waggoner, the foreman out at Madison's place . . . the Circle M, where you're headed . . . often comes in on weekends and transacts a little business. But he missed last weekend. Don't know why. Almost always he shows up on Saturday, even if he don't want to buy nothin'. We just set around, talk—like you and me are doin'—and play dominoes. You play dominoes?"

"I do," Matt replied.

"If you want, you can stay over. It'll be dark before you get halfway out there. No sense in sleepin' on the ground. I got an extra room and a bunk."

"That sounds real fine," Matt replied.

Riggs chuckled and Matt could see that a little company was a real treat for the old man. "I'll go get the dominoes," he said. As he rose, he fished in his pocket and came up with a key. He tossed it at Matt. "You can go get your gun out of the box."

# CHAPTER

# ⋆ 4 ⋆

The immense bulk of the distant Baboquivaris was playing a visual trick on Matt. The mountains rose on the
horizon with such towering dominance that they conveyed
the impression that they were much closer than they really were.

Matt studied them as he rode. The Rockies, where Matt
had traveled extensively, were awesome, no doubt about
it, but the Baboquivaris, foot for canyon foot, might well
be more torturous to navigate, Matt told himself. Old man
Riggs had said that Baboquivari Peak stood nearly eight
thousand feet high. The dark, shadowed canyons and the
steep, upthrusting slopes gave the Baboquivaris an almost
ominous character. "Lots of good timber up near the top,"
Riggs had told him, "but it'll never be harvested. No damn
way to build wagon trails into them mountains. They're too
rugged."

But stretching in an easterly direction from the base of
the mountains, the complexion of the land was entirely
different . . . mostly rolling grassland. Cleve had exagger-
ated when he said the grass was stirrup high, but he hadn't
stretched the truth too much. It was, indeed, good growth,
and Matt had every expectation that Cleve was doing well
with his cattle-ranching operation.

Occasionally, as he rode, Matt saw Circle M cattle grazing

23

on the range. All in all, the panoramic vista across the broad Altar Valley appeared tranquil and invitingly pastoral, an apparent contradiction of all of the stories he had heard about the Apache menace. But, back at Riggs's store, over dominoes, the old man had put that once deadly problem into a more current perspective. "It don't really amount to much anymore," Riggs had told him. "The reservation, the troops, and the changin' times have caused the danger to subside a great deal. The army has even enlisted Apache scouts that track down the renegades. So, most of the trouble these days comes from bad-ass malcontents and them that drink too much tiswin. And when a gang of Apache do break out, they usually head for Mexico. It's lots easier to steal horses and cattle down there. There ain't much in the way of troops in northern Mexico. So . . . they go where the raidin's easier. That's what makes it possible for your friend Madison to operate these days."

Matt hoped that Riggs was right. He had every reason to believe that the old man knew what he was talking about. Riggs had told Matt that he hadn't seen any Apache for quite a spell. "I was out huntin' one day, about three months back. Down in a deep gully and I seen 'em go by on a neighboring ridge . . . eight of 'em, comin' out of Mexico, headin' north with a few stolen horses. Those were the first I'd seen in a long time."

So Matt rode across the valley in a leisurely fashion, drinking in the scenery and looking forward to a nice string of lazy untroubled days on the Madison spread.

A little past midafternoon, at a time when the sun was nearly ready to disappear behind the high ridges of the Baboquivaris, Matt paused at a water tank to let his horse drink. Six or eight head of Cleve's cattle were grazing not far from the catchment. While the horse took its fill, Matt surveyed the broad distance between himself and the mountains. His eyeball estimation told him that he had permitted himself to drift north a bit . . . maybe by several miles or more. At least that was what the position of the peak was indicating.

Finished at the water hole, Matt moved his horse in a

southwesterly direction, on a route that finally intersected with a shallow, yet rugged canyon. On the far side of the canyon a scattering of small, rocky hills protruded up from the gentle roll of surrounding grassland. Matt rode along the rim of the canyon until he found a suitable place for the horse to descend. The canyon had been formed by endless eons of rushing water . . . water that roared down from the towering Baboquivaris during infrequent but often torrential desert thunderstorms. Now, under a cloudless sky, the canyon bottom was broad, dry, and sandy.

Since the canyon twisted in a southerly direction and the forty-foot cliffs threw shade, Matt decided to ride the bottom for a while. He let the buckskin pick its way down the side of the canyon. The burro had been left behind with Riggs, who offered to provide its keep for next to nothing. At the bottom of the canyon Matt aimed the horse in a downstream direction and kept it on the western side of the streambed, taking advantage of the shade.

After riding about two miles toward the south, Matt figured that he had put himself and his horse back on course. A narrower tributary wash joined the canyon from the west, and Matt decided to follow it until he located a good path back up to the flatlands above.

The side canyon grew narrower as he proceeded, eventually closing in until it was no more than twenty feet across. "Damn," Matt mumbled under his breath. He knew he had gotten himself into a tight box canyon that would most likely provide no way out. He turned his mount and started back.

It took Matt nearly fifteen minutes to retrace his path to the place where he had turned into the narrower gorge. He was less than fifty feet from the entrance when a high-pitched yet commanding voice called out from above: "Stop and identify yourself!"

Matt stopped as ordered and raised his eyes to a jutting ledge near the place where the sidewash joined the wider stream bed. His eyes picked out a figure, mostly in silhouette, standing on the outcropping of rock. The figure moved, ever so slightly, and a ray of sunlight danced off the barrel of a rifle held across the waist . . . held loosely, but held so it could quickly be raised to a firing position.

"My name's Matt Ramsey," he called out, his voice echoing through the narrow space between the rock walls. As soon as he had spoken his name, the figure took a quick step forward on the rocky shelf, moving out into full sunlight. The first thing Matt took notice of was the corn-silk hair . . . well past shoulder-length, billowing out on the warm canyon wind. The distance was too far for the person's features to be distinct, but Matt could plainly see the bright red cloth, wrapped Indian-style around the forehead. He noticed, too, the blue shirt and dark trousers tucked into knee-high boots. Slung across one shoulder was a bandolier of cartridges.

"Who?" the distant figure queried.

Matt's eyes narrowed and he peered at the figure more intently. Now he noticed the wasp-thin waist. Hell, he told himself, that's no man. That's a woman. "Matt Ramsey," he repeated. "I'm headin' for the Circle M Ranch."

"Stay there," the voice called back. Then the figure stepped into the shadows and disappeared.

No doubt about it, Matt told himself. The person on the ledge had been a woman. The voice, the tiny waist, and the long, blowing hair confirmed it, as far as Matt was concerned.

He waited as ordered . . . watching the opening between the cliffs where the streambeds connected . . . sitting slouched in the saddle and pondering the apparent incongruity of a woman, armed and dressed like a man, in the lonely wilderness of territorial Arizona. He knew of only one woman who lived in the Altar Valley east of the Baboquivaris. Alicia? Surely not, he told himself.

A large, dark horse being ridden at a full gallop broke Matt's train of thought as it made a sharp, sand-tossing turn into the side canyon. The figure with the billowing hair was in the saddle, one hand holding the rifle, the other the reins. The rider brought the horse to a sliding halt a few feet in front of Matt's buckskin.

She studied his face intently for several seconds. Matt

studied back. It *was* Alicia! No doubt about it. But an Alicia so transformed that only the basic features of her face remained the same. Well . . . the face *and* the contour of her ever-prominent breasts beneath the fabric of the muslin shirt.

Her once straw-colored hair was now bleached to a golden hue by the desert sun. No longer confined by pins and nets, it fanned out across her shoulders, straight and unrestrained except for the aboriginal touch of the knotted red headband. The skin of her face, deeply tanned by the sun, framed her pale blue eyes, making them appear paler than ever before . . . as pale and piercing as the eyes of a mountain cat. In her right hand she held the heavy Henry rifle with a commanding confidence. Now her voice was low. "Matt? Matt Ramsey from Texas?" she inquired.

Matt smiled. "Yes, Matt Ramsey from Texas. Nice to see you again, Alicia. I've come out to visit you and Cleve."

Suddenly a look of anguish spread across Alicia's transformed countenance. Her lips pursed for a fleeting moment, and her brow contorted with an inner pain that would almost instantly be explained by her words. "Cleve is missing," she said.

Her pain transferred itself instantly to Matt. He could feel it, and he knew it was not the minor pain of casual concern. "Disappeared? Is that what you mean?"

She nodded. "We've been looking for him for more than a week. Eleven days now. He went out to check some water holes. He never came back. His horse didn't come back. We're been out looking . . . all of us . . . every day."

"How many is all of us?" Matt wanted to know.

"All of the hands. We have four cowboys and nine Pima Indians. We've searched in every direction . . . in every gully . . . in every canyon along the foothills of the Baboquivaris." Suddenly a trickle of a tear spilled out of Alicia's right eye and ran down her cheek.

Matt chewed on his lower lip and gave the abrupt and unsettling news some thought. "Is that what you're doin' out here?" he asked. "Lookin' for him?"

She nodded, then rubbed her tear-stained cheek against

the upper sleeve of the shirt. "Today I've been up and down the big arroyo and all of the sidewashes that run into it. That's how I spotted you."

Matt, vividly remembering the skinned corpse and Riggs's long-running vendetta with the Apache, asked a logical question. "Any chance that he had a run-in with Indians?"

"That's the first thing we thought of," Alicia replied. "But if it had been Apache, they would have killed him and left him where he fell. Taken his horse, his weapons, and whatever of his personal belongings they might have wanted. But they wouldn't have gone to any trouble at all to hide or conceal his body. The boys and me all agree on that point. It wasn't Apache."

"I'll help in every way I can," said Matt. "Every way I can." But even as he spoke the words, he wondered how much help he could really provide. Missing eleven days. All of the people on the ranch scouring the countryside. It didn't look good, and Matt could feel the fear seeping through his body . . . fear that one of the best friends he had ever known was dead.

"I want to keep riding the lip of the canyon," Alicia told him. "I've been this way twice before, but I want to cover it again."

"We'll ride together, and you can fill me in," Matt replied.

Alicia led the way, sitting arrow-straight astride the big black gelding with the the Henry rifle held comfortably in the crook of her right arm. Matt's mind was a jumble of thoughts. Most of them had to do with Cleve's mysterious disappearance, but at the same time a curious and questioning part of his brain was trying to reconcile Alicia's transformation. In addition to the physical change, there was a notable difference in her inner person as well. Torn as she was by her personal crisis, Matt perceived a strength that had not been apparent in the Alicia he had met years back in east Texas. Alicia, he told himself, had become a new woman in the wilds of Arizona . . . a woman who, under even extreme pressure, could make decisions and act on them. When she turned her head and looked off to the right, Matt, riding behind, caught her bronzed face in profile. Alicia, he mused, had become almost menacingly beautiful.

They were crossing the wide expanse of the sandy primary wash when Alicia pointed to the ground with the barrel of her rifle. "Those tracks are from Manuel's horse. Two days back he rode the wash, and I stayed up above." She halted her mount, and Matt pulled up beside her.

"Who's Manuel?"

"One of our cowboys. We've been going out early, every day. We set up our routes off a map. I'm losing hope, Matt. We've covered all of our land . . . crossed and recrossed it. We've gone into the foothills of the Baboquivari . . . gone east beyond Big Brawley Wash. To the north McNeal and his hands have been searching that part of the country. But I don't trust McNeal. In fact, if we're going to consider foul play, McNeal would be my only local suspect."

They started riding again. "What about this McNeal?" Matt wanted to know.

"He has a spread larger than ours . . . borders us to the north. I've never liked him. That's part of it. Just a womanly kind of intuition, I guess. He's crude, arrogant. Knows everything. He came out from back East, and I think he's got big eastern money behind him. About seven or eight months ago he started talking to Cleve about leasing all of our land that borders and runs into the foothills of the Baboquivaris. That didn't make much sense to Cleve . . . didn't make sense to me, either. That rocky, rugged country up there wouldn't support enough cattle to make it pay. McNeal never did explain satisfactorily why he wanted to lease the foothill acreage. When Cleve said he wasn't interested, McNeal got ugly."

"He make any threats?" Matt asked.

"No. I don't mean that. He's just an ugly man with an ugly way about him. Intimidating, I guess you could say. Trying to make Cleve feel like he was foolish or stupid for turning down the offer. McNeal has his people out looking, too. He offered to cover all of the land up his way. His foreman has come by twice to give me a report. Both times it's been the same. Like us, they haven't found anything, either."

"Do you feel that McNeal is really putting an effort into it? Or is he only saying he is?"

"His foreman, Ransom Butler, is a good man . . . friend of ours, actually. If Ransom says they're out lookin', I believe him."

Once they reached the east side of the wash, Alicia guided her mount up and out of the canyon. Matt followed silently, waiting for further conversation until they were back up on the flatlands, where it would be easier to ride and talk.

It was late afternoon before they hit level ground. "We'll head into the ranch house now," said Alicia. "It'll be dark before we get back." As she spoke, she noticed that Matt's eyes were not on hers. He was looking beyond her . . . into the distance. She watched as his brow wrinkled . . . then he lowered his eyes . . . stared at the saddle horn, and rubbed his lips together. "What is it?" she inquired.

He kept his eyes lowered . . . remained silent. When he looked up, she could read the deep concern—maybe even fear—that had settled over his face like a mask. "Out there," he said, motioning with his head toward the east, "about a mile away, there's buzzards circlin'. We better go take a look."

For the first and only time that day, the hint of a smile appeared on Alicia's face. She said it very softly. "It's all right, Matt. It's all right. I was over there yesterday. It's only a calf . . . killed by a mountain lion that slipped down from the Baboquivaris." With her words relief washed over Matt's face. He smiled back. "Let's go in," she said. "Juanita will have a good meal waiting for us."

# CHAPTER

## ★ 5 ★

A nearly full moon hung in the eastern sky. Matt, with a cup of late-evening coffee in his hand, rocked easily on the long wooden porch of the Circle M ranch house. A tolerably cool breeze was blowing up the valley from the south. Nice evening, he thought . . . and a nice place to be. Cleve Madison had built himself quite a ranch . . . an impressive enterprise for a location so remote and far distanced from the avenues of frontier commerce.

Alicia had given him a partial tour of the property before dinner. The main house was single-story and nearly a hundred feet long, built of thick adobe and coated with white plaster. The covered wooden porch ran the entire length of the building. On the north end were two rooms, each with an exterior entry. The smaller room, Alicia had explained, provided living quarters for Señora Juanita Montoya and her seventeen-year-old daughter, Theresa. Plump, middle-aged Juanita served as housekeeper and cook. Theresa, her helper, was a pretty, dark-eyed girl with straight black hair and a perpetual smile.

A very large room at the far end of the building served as a bunkhouse for graying Pete Waggoner, Cleve's trusted foreman, and the three permanent cowboys. Matt had met them at dinner, and he liked them all. Pete was a lifetime cowpoke who, according to Alicia, knew everything there was to know about running a cattle ranch. Bob Whipple, not yet twenty-one, had come out from Texas with Cleve and Alicia . . . a sawmill worker turned cowboy. Manuel Garza and Jose Escobar were seasoned Mexican hands hired by Cleve in Tucson.

After a huge meal that combined both traditional American food and Juanita's Mexican dishes, Alicia had shown Matt the large adobe barn . . . the corrals . . . and finally the group of small adobe outbuildings that housed the Pima Indians. There were nine of them, all male and varying in age from a young teenager to a stooped but sinewy man with shoulder-length white hair. "They are shy and very gentle people," Alicia told Matt. "But they are not entirely passive. If threatened, they are fierce fighters." She introduced Matt to several of them. Later she told Matt, "They are good workers, very loyal . . . but quite superstitious and easily frightened. They are disturbed by Cleve's disappearance."

The main portion of the ranch house contained five large bedrooms, all opening onto a common hallway that ran from the big sitting room to the south end of the building. Alicia had given Matt a place at the end of the hall . . . a cheerful room with curtains and a nicely made double bed. "This one has windows on two sides," Alicia told him. "You'll need all the breeze you can get."

It was all very nice, Matt told himself as he sat on the porch and rocked. Almost perfect. But it wasn't something he could enjoy . . . not now . . . not with his best friend missing. Matt Ramsey wasn't a pessimistic man, but he had serious doubts that Cleve Madison would ever turn up alive. Not likely, not likely at all. But he had no intention of sharing that thought with Alicia. So he sat . . . rocked . . . and looked up at the bright slice of moon and tried to examine the problem from every hypothetical angle.

He rocked until the coffee left in the mug was no longer warm. He leaned forward and tossed what was left into the yard. At the far end of the building a door opened and light from inside was cast across the porch. A figure stepped out, closed the door, and walked Matt's way.

It was Pete Waggoner. "Nice night, ain't it?" said Pete.

"It is," replied Matt. Pete eased into a nearby rocker, leaned back, and lit a pipe. "I thought maybe Alicia would join me here on the porch," said Matt. "Does she go to bed early?"

Pete rocked for a few moments before replying. "No." He rocked some more before going on. "In fact, as far as I know, she don't go to bed at all. She's gone out again. Searchin' in the dark. She's been doin' it every night. She rides all day, comes back and eats . . . then goes out again." Pete shook his head slowly. "She's gonna cave in soon."

"She doesn't sleep at all?" asked Matt.

"I s'pose some . . . maybe a couple of hours. We don't know. But we know for sure she stays out past the time we all drop off. When she returns, none of us knows. Then, come breakfast time, she's out in the kitchen. She eats a few bites, then goes over the map with us . . . assigns routes for each of us . . . then she's off again."

"I guess I can understand what's drivin' her," said Matt. "I'm sure it's the confusion of not knowin'."

"Without a doubt," replied Pete. "And it gets worse with each passing day. Sometimes I wonder how it will ever end . . . this searchin' and lookin', I mean."

Matt leaned forward, elbows on knees. He looked directly at Pete. "I got to say this, Pete. . . . My best thinkin' tells me that most likely he's dead."

Pete nodded thoughtfully. "Yes . . . most likely. But that won't stop her from lookin'. And as long as she looks . . . so will the rest of us."

"Alicia told me that if Apache killed him, they would leave him lay."

"They would," replied Pete.

"Wouldn't any other kind of rovin' bandit do the same? I hear that sometimes Mexican bandits drift up this way from down below the border. But if it was a Mexican bandit— someone just passin' through that killed him—why would he bother to haul him off and hide the body?"

"Gringo bandit the same," said Pete. "He'd kill his victim, take what he wanted, and ride on. No need to try to cover it up since he'd be long gone before the body was found."

"So," said Matt, "that rules out Apache and bandits. What about this rancher, McNeal?"

Pete took a long draw on his pipe. "I doubt it," he replied. "McNeal is a common asshole . . . an order taker for some back-East millionaires. But I don't get the feeling he has murder in him. But, then again . . . who knows?"

"Accident?" queried Matt.

"Cleve had four water holes to check out that day . . . a round-trip ride of about twenty miles. But the route was over easy, open ground. What kind of an accident could he have had? Hell, I've tried and I can't come up with any type of accident that would've gotten both him and the horse. And if it hadn't of gotten the horse, the horse would've come back. On the other hand, if Cleve had been in rough country—bad country, like the canyons up in the Baboquivaris—then I can see it. Maybe a rockslide . . . or maybe the horse slips off a cliff. But, hell, he wasn't in that kind of country."

"I tend to go along with you about an accident," said Matt. "But if we take the position that an accident isn't what got Cleve, then it has to be foul play. Some kind of foul play."

Pete sat silently for a long time. Finally he tapped out the pipe and spoke. "It's drivin' us bats, isn't it? If it's drivin' us bats, what do you think it's doin' to her?" He rose slowly from the chair. "I need some sleep. You goin' in?"

Matt thought about it for a moment. "No," he said. "I'm goin' to stay here . . . wait for her to come in. Someone needs to talk to her about this ridin' out at night."

# CHAPTER

## ★ 6 ★

Alicia had agreed with Matt concerning her late-night search-ing. "I know it's not wise," she told him. "I'll be the first to admit that it's probably dangerous, and there's very little I can see in the dark. But . . ." and at that point, her voice had dropped into silence.

"I know why you're going out," Matt told her softly and gently. "I'd probably be doin' the same if I was you. But in the long run it's only goin' to wear you down . . . break you eventually."

Then she cried, softly but for a long time. "I think I could take it better if I knew he was dead. If only I knew . . . something . . . anything . . . it would be better than this. Not a sign, not a clue to what happened."

Nevertheless, Alicia started staying at the ranch after sundown, often sitting on the porch with Matt, sipping her evening coffee and staring into the darkness . . . listening to the mournful distant wail of night-hunting coyotes.

Although Alicia remained at the ranch through the night, Matt had to wonder if she was actually getting much sleep. Not likely, he conjectured. Each morning when he made his way to the kitchen for his first cup of morning coffee, Alicia was there ahead of him, fully dressed and ready to commence another day of looking for her lost hus-band.

On a bright and cloudless Thursday, four days after his arrival, Matt stepped into the dimly lit dining room just as the first rays of light were appearing in the east. He saw her sitting at her place, her forehead resting on her folded hands . . . a cup of untouched coffee nearby.

Wearily, as his bootheels announced arrival, she raised her eyes to meet his. Something in her look told Matt that another burden had been added to her deep concern over Cleve's disappearance.

"Morning," she said, trying to smile. Ordinarily Matt would have gone on to the kitchen, drawn by the aroma of Juanita's coffee, but instead, he stopped and gave her a long look.

"You feelin' all right?" Matt inquired.

She sighed heavily. "The Indians have left."

"All of them?" Matt asked.

She nodded her head in the affirmative. "I'm not surprised. Days back, Juanita told me that they were starting to get edgy. They feel that Cleve's disappearance without a trace might indicate the presence of a demon . . . a devil . . . I'm not completely sure what. Anyway, I guess it finally spooked them so bad, they just up and left."

"Can you get 'em to come back?"

"I don't even know where they've gone . . . . Most likely back to their people. This means that I'm going to have to take the other hands off the search . . . at least for some of the time."

"I'll help all I can," Matt told her.

"For the next few days I'm going to let the cowboys catch up on work. I know Cleve would have wanted it that way. No matter what, he wouldn't have wanted the ranch to fall apart. I'm thinking that you and I will do the looking . . . if you're willing."

Matt told her that of course he was willing, and that morning, as they had on all the previous mornings since his arrival, they set out even before the early sun had fully cleared the distant horizon. This particular morning, they struck a path to the north . . . riding about a half mile apart.

Matt let Alicia do the planning, such as it was. Why not? he told himself. One direction would be as good as any other. On this day Alicia's rationale made as much sense as any other decision would have made. "It seems we've covered every inch of ground toward the south . . . the direction in which he went on the day he disappeared. Maybe—just maybe—he went north. Maybe, for some reason, he decided to head north."

"Have you looked up that way before?" Matt wanted to know.

"We have," she replied, "but not as much as we have toward the south. Let's try the rugged country in the foothills today."

And so they had. Alicia, because she was more familiar with the land, took the higher ground . . . the steep foothills of the Baboquivaris. Matt rode the edge of the valley at the base, where countless little ragged arroyos, bone dry and usually no more than ten or twelve feet across, snaked their way out into the grassland. Always they were bordered on both sides by thick growth . . . mesquite trees and an uncountable variety of shrubs and desert bushes.

It would be impossible, Matt told himself . . . well, damn near impossible . . . to cover every foot of ground in the area. Each little arroyo—and there were certainly hundreds of them—was many miles in length. Each twisted and turned in such a way that a man would have to ride every foot of sandy streambed to make a complete and thorough search. A man's body could lie undiscovered until there was nothing left but bones. And then, if a sudden cloudburst came and the arroyos ran wildly, the bones could be forever buried under the shifting sand.

Still, Matt told himself, he would have to ride with Alicia for as long as she wanted to continue the search. He felt that eventually her wifely instinct . . . her deep concern . . . would be overridden by some form of natural acceptance. The kind of acceptance that comes when a person watches the slow, inexorable decline of an ill and aging relative. At any rate, at some point in time Alicia would have to give it all up. Matt wasn't sure how long that would be. By now

Cleve Madison had been gone for better than two weeks.

At midmorning Matt saw Alicia sitting her horse on a promontory several hundred feet above his own position and slightly to the north. She waved to him, then turned her mount and headed down a rocky, cacti-covered ridge.

Matt angled his buckskin in her direction, and they met on open ground in a clearing that was rimmed on three sides by a brushy growth of mesquite.

"Thought we could take a rest, if you want," she said as she rode up.

"Good idea," Matt replied.

Alicia opened a saddlebag and removed a parcel of food wrapped in cloth. She handed it to Matt. "Let's try some of Juanita's cold beef burritos." Then she untied a ground cloth from behind her saddle and spread it on the ground. Matt hoisted a water flask from his own saddle horn.

After Alicia had spread the ground cloth, she gave Matt a soft smile. "Sit," she said. "We can have a back-home type picnic." She opened the cloth and held it out to Matt. "You ever had one of these before?"

"No," he said as he took one of the burritos, "but so far I've got no complaint with anything Juanita's cooked up."

"It's shredded beef mixed with chili and beans, all wrapped in a soft flour tortilla."

Off in the distance a quail called softly. Hordes of honey-bees buzzed through the flowering mesquites. Otherwise, the little clearing was engulfed in the tranquil silence of the lonely desert. The morning was warming, but it wouldn't be actually hot until noon. Matt passed the water to Alicia. He watched her as she tipped her head back and drank. She had a bothersome beauty about her, Matt told himself. He gave his old friend Cleve credit where credit was due. Cleve had seen something in the old Alicia that had totally escaped Matt. Then Cleve had brought her to the Arizona wilderness and let the magical transformation, which surely only he could have foreseen, take place. Bothersome beauty. The thought repeated itself in Matt's mind. A trickle of water spilled out of the mouth of the flask and ran down her chin, the droplets cascading between the open collar of her shirt and into the soft crevasse between her breasts.

She lowered the canteen and wiped her mouth on the sleeve of her denim shirt. "Cleve and I used to do this a lot. Ride out to inspect the range . . . find a nice place to stop." She paused and looked directly into Matt's eyes. "You didn't like me when you first met me back in Texas, did you?"

Matt smiled softly . . . finished chewing. "If I lied, you'd know I was lyin'. Truth to tell, my impression was that you were . . ." He paused, searching for the right word or words.

She helped him. "Frumpy, dull, restrained, sour on life. How about cheerless?"

His smile broadened. "No need to be so hard on yourself. But you have changed a lot."

"Cleve rescued me from a world so dreary that I couldn't truly describe what it was like. My home and the town around us was so steeped in its dull traditions that I saw myself as a prisoner of dullness. Everything that everybody did was done because someone else generations back, I suppose, had said how it was to be done. It was a rigid, ritualistic way of life . . . especially difficult for a young woman . . . for a woman of any age. I could look at my own mother and all the other females of her generation and see nothing but all-consuming dullness. And I resigned myself to the dullness and permitted myself to become as dull as all the others. I had no spirit, Matt. In time I, like all the other women in that town, would have become nothing more than a dull, slow-moving body without any spirit at all. Cleve saved me from that. And for that and all of his good qualities, I love him with a depth that would be impossible to explain."

"No need to explain," said Matt. "You are changed. When you came pounding into that gully . . . ridin' up with that big rifle in the crook of your arm and your hair blowin' in the wind . . . I was truly taken aback. I knew it was you, but at the same time I knew it wasn't the you I had met in Texas. You're a beautiful woman, and it's hurtin' me a lot to see you hurtin'."

He thought he could see a tear forming in the corner of her eye. She spoke softly. "I'm so glad you're here. The words *heaven-sent* cross my mind. You're here when we need you. I'm so grateful to you, Matt."

After that they sat quietly for a while, eating . . . resting . . . taking in and being soothed by the awesome beauty of the country around them. Finally, finished with their food, Matt broke the silence. "Think we should head on?"

She smiled and got to her feet. Matt rolled the ground cloth and placed it back where it belonged behind Alicia's saddle. As he was tying it in place, she moved close to him, placing the wrapped and remaining food into the saddlebag. Finished, she laid her forehead against the saddle leather and began crying. Matt watched uncomfortably as he finished securing the ground cloth. Then he reached out and placed his hand on her shoulder. At his touch she turned to him . . . clutched his arms and buried her face against his chest. He held her until she had cried herself out. When she was finished, she tilted her head up . . . looked into his face and smiled . . . squeezed his arms with her hands. "Thank you," she said very softly. "We better ride."

They continued their search through the balance of the morning and into the afternoon. Discovered nothing. When they next stopped to rest, it was in the lee of a cliff that threw welcome shade against the rising temperature. They sat on flat rocks and drank from their water flasks.

"Let's circle back," said Alicia. "Ride east out into the valley to the big wash that runs due south. I'll work one side, you the other."

"Sounds fine," Matt replied.

After a few moments of quiet she spoke again. "Let me ask you, Matt . . . have you considered the possibility that Cleve might have simply ridden away? Just left?"

Matt nodded his head slowly. "I have. But only because that's one of the possibilities. Were things good between the two of you?"

"Yes. Very good. Truly, Matt, I can't imagine any two people being more satisfied and happy with each other than Cleve and I." She paused for a moment. "But still,

I must confront that possibility . . . that for some reason he just rode away. My God, Matt, we've looked everywhere."

"I know," he replied. "Every day, as we ride, I try to consider every possibility in my own mind, just as you do. I try to list them in some kind of order . . . the most likely first. To me the most likely is an accident. But unless he was in very rugged country—where you say he wouldn't or shouldn't have been—an accident wouldn't have gotten both him and the horse. The only thing that would have gotten both of 'em would have been falling off of some high cliff."

"We could look forever in the Baboquivaris," Alicia said. "Besides, I feel sure he didn't go in there. No reason at all."

"Then," said Matt, "the possibility that he was harmed by another person . . . or persons."

"Killed," she said.

"Yes, killed. If it was bandits or Apache, they would have left him. Even if they buried him, they wouldn't have buried the horse."

"Unless it was somebody who wanted him done away with."

"Like McNeal? Only you said you felt strongly that McNeal is not the killin' kind."

"I even considered our foreman, Pete. That's absurd. The other cowboys . . . also absurd."

"At any rate, the last on my list is Cleve ridin' away of his own free will. Men sometimes do that . . . get strange in the head and just disappear. But still, that's last on my list. However, he could have left against his wishes. Maybe Apache or bandits took him away."

"Why?"

"I wouldn't have the foggiest idea . . . none whatsoever. But still, it's a possibility." Matt did not mention to Alicia the fact that for one quick, fleeting moment a few days back he had momentarily considered the unthinkable possibility that she might have done away with her husband. But Matt had been with her and watched her day after long day, and he knew beyond a shadow of a doubt that her grief and fearsome concern were real. He was so sure of that that he actually chided himself for having let such a thought enter his mind . . . for even a moment.

# CHAPTER

## ★ 7 ★

By midafternoon the temperature in the Altar Valley had risen to an even one hundred degrees, but a soft breeze from the north and the almost total absence of humidity made riding the flatland a tolerable exercise. From time to time Matt was tempted to let his eyelids drop shut, permitting him to take a short siesta in the saddle. But he fought against the urge and scanned the countryside around him in fading hope that he might perceive at least a shred of evidence that could be used to unravel the mystery of Cleve Madison's disappearance.

By the time the brilliant orb of sun had moved to a position just above the jagged peaks of the Baboquivari, Matt was starting to feel saddle-weary. He looked across the wide wash to the place where Alicia was riding. Apparently, she intended to continue the search until the shadows deepened into dusk. That was the way it had been each day that Matt had gone out with her.

Finally Matt hit a stretch of land that was stove-top flat. He could see all the way to the horizon and there was nothing out there. So he turned his horse to the west, crossed the wide wash, and joined Alicia.

"Nothing, as usual," she said with a trace of resignation in her voice.

Matt didn't know what to say, so he said nothing. They

rode in silence for nearly a mile. Suddenly Alicia reined her mount . . . stood in the stirrups and shielded her eyes from the sun. She pointed. "Someone's riding this way," she said.

Matt followed the direction of her pointing finger.

"Movin' at a gallop, too," he remarked.

"Let's see who it is," Alicia said, flicking the reins and touching her mount with the spurs.

After they had closed the distance to less than a quarter mile, Alicia let the black gelding ease back into a walk. "It's Theresa, Juanita's daughter. Hope nothing else has gone wrong."

Theresa continued at a gallop . . . finally pulled her horse to a halt in front of Matt and Alicia. Even through the swirling dust, they could see the wide smile on her attractive face. Thank God, no more trouble, thought Matt.

"We have a visitor, señora. A very distinguished visitor!"

Alicia knew instantly that the pretty Theresa was attempting to lift her spirits with the announcement, but it really wasn't working. Truth to tell, Alicia's heart had started pounding furiously at the sight of the approaching rider . . . hoping that a message of Cleve was being delivered. Nevertheless, she appreciated Theresa's effort. "And who might the visitor be?" inquired Alicia.

"A priest," said Theresa. "A black robe . . . a Jesuit priest traveling through our land on a special quest." Of course, to young Theresa, a lifelong and devout Catholic, a visit from a passing priest meant more than it did to the troubled Alicia. "Mama put him in the big room just off the porch. She said she knew that you would have it that way."

Now Alicia did smile. "Yes," she replied, "that's exactly what I would have wanted her to do. And I suppose she's planning a special meal as well."

Theresa's face broke into a broad and radiant grin, her dark eyes flashing. "Sí, señora, she told the cowboys to shave their faces and wear clean shirts."

Alicia looked across at Matt with two days' stubble

on his face. "I'll bet that means you, too," said Alicia. Matt gave her a crooked grin. "Ride with us, Theresa, unless you feel you need to hurry back. Matt and I are going to take it slow. We've been in these saddles all day."

"I'll ride along with you a short distance . . . let my horse rest a little. Then I must, indeed, hurry back. So much to do!"

Then the three of them, through the shadows that had marched out from the base of the Baboquivaris, rode at a walk through the Madison grassland. After they had covered a distance of nearly a mile, young Theresa announced her intent to pick up the pace in order to return and help her mother.

"You said the priest was on a quest," said Alicia. "Did he say what kind of a quest?"

"*Sí*," replied Theresa. "He says that he is seeking permission from the owner of this land to travel into the Baboquivaris to search for a lost mission. A mission built long ago by the Jesuits and then abandoned after many Indian raids."

"Very interesting," said Alicia. "Now, hurry along. Juanita will be needing your help. Tell her to set the table with my wedding silver."

Theresa grinned again. "She anticipated your request. I have already polished it." Then the Mexican girl slapped her mount across the flanks with the reins and rode off at a gallop.

As her figure diminished into the distance, Alicia turned to Matt. "I've never entertained a priest . . . a few Baptist ministers back in Texas . . . but never a priest."

"Well," replied Matt, "I hear they put their britches on the same as any other man."

For the first time that day Alicia broke forth with a laugh. "They wear robes, dear Matt."

Her laugh raised Matt's spirits just a little. He was happy to see Alicia laugh. "I'll bet that under the robes they wear britches."

Now she smiled broadly. "That might be a hard bet to

prove. Sort of like trying to find out what a Scotsman wears under his kilts."

"Probably so. But I have a feelin' that our distinguished visitor isn't all that much different from common folks like us."

"That's not what people like Juanita and Theresa think. They seem, at times, almost awestruck by their priests. They place them on a very high pedestal. And perhaps that's the way it should be."

Deep shadows now stretched clear across the broad valley. Weariness and the apparent end of day seemed to curtail their conversation, and they rode on in silence. Matt was not an especially religious man . . . hadn't been in a church on a regular basis for many years . . . yet he believed in a caring God. Perhaps, he told himself, there was reason for the priest's arrival. Maybe there was a purpose in his visit that would be revealed. Perhaps. And, then again, perhaps not.

# CHAPTER

## ★ 8 ★

Juanita did indeed prepare an impressive dinner for the newly arrived guest who, upon Alicia's arrival, introduced himself as Father Silvestre Velez Arredondo, a Jesuit priest from the mission of Caborca located approximately a hundred miles below the Mexican border in the vicinity of the Rio Magdalena.

Juanita and Theresa appeared delighted to serve the black-robed priest. Juanita hovered over his shoulder like a protective mother hen, while Theresa darted back and forth to the kitchen, eyes bashfully averted, bringing an almost endless offering of delicacies.

Matt viewed the entire proceeding with an almost detached amusement. The four cowboys, apparently uncomfortable in their "go-to-town" pressed shirts, ate heartily but self-consciously. Most of the evening's conversation was between Alicia and the good Father.

He was a man in his mid- or late-thirties, of medium stature with a light Castilian complexion and deep-set eyes. His English was good but laced with the expected accent. Father Arredondo did not smile but seemed a serious man on what was to him apparently serious business. However, he was also a man of good manners and for the earlier part of the evening, he spoke softly to Alicia about his sympathy and concern for her vanished husband.

"Sometimes it is most difficult to understand God's will and God's way," he told her. And all the while, as he spoke, Juanita nodded silently in agreement with his every syllable. "This plan of God is so all-encompassing and so totally glorious and so totally beyond the comprehension of the average person that we sometimes lose sight of the irrefutable fact that nothing—absolutely nothing—is random. Everything is for a purpose, and everything is part of this magnificent tapestry of the heavenly plan."

But after he had taken an ample amount of time to console Alicia, the priest turned conversation to the business of his quest. Over a course of thinly sliced, marinated, and gently broiled beef filets, Arredondo provided the details of his trip into the territory of Arizona. "There is," he said, "a network of Spanish missions throughout northern Mexico and extending west across both Arizona and California. Some of the missions are very old . . . some built more than two hundred years ago. Many of them are still operating. For example, the gorgeous mission of San Xavier del Bac, located about sixty miles north of your ranch, serves the Indians and settlers in the area of the Pueblo of Tucson."

"I've seen San Xavier," Alicia cut in. "My husband and I visited it on a trip to Tucson. Very inspiring."

Father Arredondo dabbed at the corner of his mouth and watched as hovering Juanita filled his wineglass. "On the other hand," he continued, "some of the missions have been abandoned. For example, the mission of Tumacacori, only twenty-five miles to the east of you in the deserted village of Tubac. That mission was never completed because of Mexico's successful war for independence. Without the support and money of the king of Spain, work had to be stopped."

"And I've seen that one," Matt interjected. "I passed through Tubac on my way out here just a few days back. The old mission is, as you said, deserted. No doors . . . no windows . . . with its bell tower unfinished."

"And most likely, it will always remain that way," he said. He paused to push his empty plate away. Juanita signaled to Theresa, who started toward the priest with a steaming platter. But he waved her aside and went on. "However, let me explain the nature of my business north of the border. A few of these old missions have literally become lost . . . no longer exist . . . except, perhaps, in some cases a few crumbling walls. It is my assignment to locate the sites of several of these old missions. Once that has been accomplished, the church will, at some later date, build commemorative monuments at the sites."

"And," said Alicia, "one of those sites is near here. Am I correct?"

"Precisely so," replied the priest. "Quite likely on land that you own. At the very least I would have to pass through your property in order to reach it. This site I am seeking was once the location of a small establishment known as the mission of San Acacia del Norte . . . built in the vastness of the Baboquivari Mountains just to the west."

"That's pretty rough country," interjected the foreman, Pete Waggoner. "Seems a strange place to build a mission."

The priest nodded rather solemnly. "*Sí* . . . established by a small group of Jesuits who desired total solitude and the opportunity to serve the simple and peaceful Indians of the region. But after a period of time the fierce Apache, claiming the area as their sacred ground, launched attack after attack on San Acacia. Finally, in a massive raid, all of the priests were murdered, and the peaceful Indians retreated back into the deep canyons. The Apache tore down the mission . . . hauled every last block and beam away . . . and restored the land to its original condition."

Matt was intrigued by the story. "In that case it would be hard to find . . . hard to confirm where the mission was actually located."

"Except for one strong piece of evidence. Sometime after the final Apache attack, an Indian—a Pima from the region, who had been baptized at San Acacia—traveled to San Xavier del Bac and gave a report on the massacre. He told the church authorities that the Apache had great difficulty in hauling away the mission bell, which weighed nearly a ton. The Pima said that the bell was dragged by many Apache to a ravine . . . five hundred and forty paces, he said, south of the mission . . . and there it was shoved over the edge of the arroyo."

Pete Waggoner offered a thought. "If it weighed that much, it's probably lyin' right where they dumped it. Even torrential rain wouldn't move an object that heavy."

"Precisely," replied Father Arredondo. "So, with old maps of the region, found in our archives, and with the location of the bell, as supplied by the Pima, I think my chances for locating San Acacia del Norte are quite good. But," he went on, "I feel obligated to seek your permission to embark on my search."

Alicia smiled softly. "That's a very modest request. I give you my permission . . . although above the foothills the land does not actually belong to my husband and me. You are free to travel as you wish . . . and you are invited to use the ranch house as headquarters during your search. The room you are now occupying will be kept for you."

The priest nodded thoughtfully. "Very kind of you. So . . . now I must excuse myself. As with all priests, I must spend the balance of this long day attending to spiritual matters." He pushed his chair back. "I intend to set out early in the morning. Perhaps"—and he turned toward Juanita—"you would make a small donation of food supplies."

Juanita beamed. "By all means, Father. It would be an honor."

Alicia spoke up. "One other thing, Father. I am going to insist that one of my men accompany you into the mountains." She turned toward young Bob Whipple and gestured in his direction. "Bob is one of the most dependable ranch hands you could ever find. He's an expert with horses and has been into the Baboquivaris many times."

The priest shook his head vigorously. "Not necessary. No. No. I am used to riding the lonely trail."

Alicia smiled. "Remember, Father, you asked my permission. Permission is granted on the basis that you have an armed escort to go with you."

"I prefer to travel alone," the priest replied.

"The Baboquivaris are not only rugged. They're deceptive. It's easy to get lost in there."

"It is not necessary," the priest repeated.

But Alicia was firm. "Please remember, Father, that we are, right now, searching for one missing person—my husband. The burden of that problem is almost more than I can tolerate. I simply cannot be a party to your going alone into those canyons."

The priest wrinkled his brow . . . paused in thought. Finally he spoke. "Well . . . if there is no other way. . . ." He paused again. "Very well."

After the priest had taken his leave, the others shoved back their chairs and congratulated Juanita and Theresa on the magnificent meal. "I'm going to help you in the kitchen," Alicia told the two women. "You've done too much already."

The men, in recognition of Juanita's hard work, helped clear the table. Then they wandered out onto the wide porch. Shortly, Pete, young Bob Whipple, and Manuel Garza headed for the big room that served as the bunkhouse.

That left only Matt and José Escobar on the porch . . . Jose puffing on a small Mexican cigar. Matt, sitting on the porch railing, watched him as he smoked. Matt liked all the hands on the Madison ranch. Cleve had done well in picking his men. José, Matt surmised, was just short of thirty . . . never been married. From earlier conversations Matt knew that he had been born in El Paso, Texas. After leaving home he had slowly drifted west, working always on cattle ranches. José was an animated young man who seemed to enjoy taking part in good conversation and swapping stories.

José removed the cigar from his lips, flicked an ash, and turned toward Matt. "Well, Señor Matt, what do you think of our visitor?"

Matt thought about it for a long moment. Finally, "Don't know as I have much of an opinion about that. Never spent much time around men of the cloth. Guess I feel just a tad uncomfortable. But that's my problem, not his."

José took another puff on the cigar. In the distance a

coyote yipped. From another place a long mournful call came back. "I am a good Catholic . . . at least, I hope I am," said José. "I take the Sacraments as often as I can. But out here in the sticks it's very difficult to fulfill all of the obligations. I tell you that so you won't think I have any prejudice against priests—particularly against Jesuit priests. All I have ever known worked hard in the service of God. But . . ." He paused for another drag on the cigar. "In the distant past . . . Jesuits developed a bad name in these parts."

"How's that?" inquired Matt.

"Some of them became tainted. My grandfather says they became victimized by gold fever. It is a well-known fact that some of the black robes, in league with Spanish soldiers, actually enslaved the Indians and forced them to mine the rich gold and silver deposits in this part of the world. Vast amounts of treasure were acquired by the black robes. It is said that many of the missions had carefully hidden, secret vaults that were used to store the gold. Tons of it, they say."

"But the priests are no longer involved in these minin' operations . . . is that what you are sayin'?"

"*Sí.* That was an old practice from days long gone by. Yet, as the priest was talkin' tonight, I couldn't help but wonder. You know what I mean?"

Matt laughed softly. "I was bit by gold fever. In fact, I spent nearly two years of my life seekin' riches in the goldfields. Maybe that's what you're comin' down with, José. Thinkin' about those stories told by your grandfather. Thinkin' about that lost mission. Thinkin' that maybe there's a secret vault. Eh?"

"No, señor. I am not a foolish man. I wouldn't waste good shoe leather wanderin' around in the wilds looking for treasure. But . . . I am simply wonderin' exactly what it is that the good priest is really lookin' for."

"It's funny," said Matt, "what a mental picture of gold can do to a man's thinkin'. I know what it can do. But, truth to tell, I've got more on my mind right now than I can comfortably handle."

"Oh, yes," replied José. "This business about Señor Madison is causin' all of us to lose sleep. We all feel very bad for Señora Madison."

"Tell me," inquired Matt, "what do you think happened to my friend Cleve? Surely you've thought about it a lot."

"Nearly every evenin' all of us hands talk about it. It is a puzzle that none of us can figure out."

"But if you had to guess . . . had to bet . . . what would you put your money on?"

"Some days I think one thing . . . the next day another. But the one possibility that keeps hangin' around is that he rode away. If it had been anything else, I just feel sure that something—some tiny piece of evidence—would have turned up. Then I ask myself why he would leave. No answer . . . none at all. But if it's drivin' me and the other boys crazy, I can imagine what it's doin' to Señora Madison."

"Did you feel that the Madisons were a happy couple . . . happy with life and each other?"

"Oh, sure," said José. "You could see that in their faces all the time. Always treatin' each other real decent. They shared in everything they did . . . shared in all the work."

Matt thought about José's reply for a moment. "So. No reason for the man to leave. Yet, I share your feeling—I mean about him ridin' away. Is it even remotely possible that Apache captured him?"

José shook his head in the negative. "No. Apache would have killed him. Sometimes Apache take young children . . . take them back to their camps and raise them as Apache. But not a grown man."

The two of them were silent for a time, Matt looking up at a sliver of transient cloud that was passing across the face of the moon. Finally he spoke. "You know old man Riggs over at Tubac?"

"I do," José replied.

"I stopped there on my way out. He seems well acquainted with Cleve and Mrs. Madison. Spoke of Pete, your foreman, too. But he made no mention of seein' Cleve lately. I'm thinkin' that if Cleve had left of his own accord, he would

have gone to Tubac to pick up supplies. He had nothin'
with him when he left, did he?"

"No," said José. "I was at the corral on the mornin' he
rode out. He might have had a little bit of food . . . just for
the day. No bedroll . . . nothin' at all that I could see."

"So . . . a man pullin' out would have to stop someplace
for supplies . . . and Riggs's place is the only place in the
whole area where a person could get supplies . . . right?"

"That's right," José replied.

"Tomorrow mornin' I'm ridin' over to Tubac and speak
to Riggs. Find out when last he saw Cleve . . . or if he's had
any other visitors lately that might throw some light on this
thing."

"That's a good idea," said José. "As good as any, I guess.
I might as well tell you that sometimes my feelin's go in
exactly the opposite direction. I get a real strong feelin' that
he's dead."

Matt considered the cowboy's statement, then replied.
"Maybe it isn't one or the other. Maybe it's both. Maybe
he rode off *and* he's dead. Who knows?"

# CHAPTER

## ★ 9 ★

As usual, the entire household at Madison's Circle M Ranch was up, dressed, fed, and in a semblance of motion shortly after first light. Matt and young Bob Whipple were lingering at the table longer than the rest . . . wiping plates dry with morning biscuits and finishing a final cup of coffee. Pete and the two Mexican hands had left the table early since they were faced with a full day's work building a new section of corral just north of the ranch house. Alicia, also, had finished quickly and was in the kitchen with Juanita pulling together several days' supplies for the priest and young Bob.

Just as Matt was taking his last sip of coffee, Father Arredondo, the last to arrive for breakfast, made his appearance. He nodded courteously to Matt and Bob . . . spoke softly. "Good morning. You had a good night's rest, I trust?"

"Did indeed," Matt replied. "And you, Father?"

For the first time the priest evidenced a slight smile. "Yes. The big bed was true luxury compared to my usual resting place on the hard ground."

Apparently, the priest's voice had carried to the kitchen. Juanita, all smiles, appeared in the doorway with a large mug of steaming coffee, which she placed at the head of the table. "Sit here, Father I'll have you some breakfast in a moment."

She stood to the side and waited until the priest had taken his seat. Then she spoke again. "We were wondering, my daughter and I, if you could say Mass for us this morning before you leave." Arredondo did not answer immediately but sat as though in deep thought. Juanita went on. "Being so far from a town or a church, we seldom have the opportunity to receive Communion."

The priest's brow knotted slightly. He cleared his throat. "There is a small problem," he said. "You see, the church gives me dispensation from many of my obligations . . . because I am so far from civilization and all other people . . . wandering alone, as it were." Now Juanita's brow knotted, too. Matt, with the nearly empty cup in his hand, watched the scene with only a casual amount of curiosity. The priest spoke again. "I have nothing with me. I carry only the barest essentials."

Juanita bent forward so she could look directly into the priest's eyes. "If I could provide some wine and a few crusts of bread . . . Under the circumstances, would that not be permissible?"

Father Arredondo rubbed his lips together . . . looked up at Matt. Matt looked back. The priest took a deep breath, let it out slowly. "Yes," he said, "under the circumstances, I feel we could do that. But we must be brief, because I need to leave early and ride a full day."

Juanita nodded her understanding and scurried into the kitchen. Even before Matt and Bob Whipple had risen from the table and picked up their plates and utensils, Juanita was back with a goblet of red wine in one hand and a small plate with torn sections of bread in the other. Theresa was right behind her.

Matt and Bob traded glances, then quietly eased out of the dining room and entered the kitchen with their dirty dishes. Alicia turned from a table where she was arranging parcels of food. "Morning," she said. Matt and Bob returned the greeting. "Bob," she said, "I want you to take good care of the padre. And take good care of yourself, too. I've got enough together here for three or four days. I'm sure you'll be coming back in by then."

Bob raised an eyebrow. "What if he don't want to come back in? What if he wants to just stay in the mountains and live off the land? I've heard that them padres can live off practically nothin' . . . just seeds and nuts . . . stuff like that."

Alicia smiled. "He told me that he would be back in no more than four days. If he decides to stay . . . well, maybe you could cultivate a taste for seeds and nuts."

Bob knew she was kidding. He returned the smile.

Matt spoke to Alicia. "You gonna ride east with me?"

"I planned on it . . . if you're still going into Tubac to see Riggs. I'll go with you as far as the point of rocks, then swing south and spend the day looking over in that area. You'll stay the night in Tubac, won't you?"

"That's what I figured on."

Shortly, Matt and Bob left for the corral to ready the horses. Juanita and Theresa returned to the kitchen with radiant looks on their faces . . . obviously pleased that Father Arredondo had taken the time to serve them the Sacraments. Alicia finished preparing provisions. Juanita fed the priest, and by seven A.M. two parties rode out from the ranch . . . the priest and Bob Whipple heading west into the Baboquivaris, and Alicia and Matt riding east toward Tubac.

After riding for nearly four hours, Matt and Alicia arrived at the point of rocks . . . a jutting little hill composed of tossed boulders and a few tenacious saguaro cacti. There they parted company as Alicia turned south, intending to make a wide circle that would place her back at the ranch by sunset.

Matt rode on . . . actually relieved to be away from other people for a while. Ever since he had arrived at the Madison ranch his mind had been almost totally occupied with the riddle of Cleve's disappearance, and he had very nearly talked himself out on the subject. There really wasn't any more to think about or talk about. Turning it over in your mind hasn't produced any results at all, he told himself. Thinkin' won't work this problem out . . . only action and time. And he was taking the action he thought most proper—going into Tubac and talk to old man Riggs. Tomorrow morning he would head north and west and visit the McNeal spread . . . maybe have an opportunity to check out rancher McNeal in person . . . at least get an up-to-date report on what, if anything, McNeal's searching cowhands had uncovered.

About three o'clock in the hot afternoon Matt was approaching another of the innumerable dry arroyos that crisscrossed the Madison property. The line of brushy mesquite trees was thicker and taller than that at most of the washes, this telling Matt that he was coming upon a major tributary for the infrequent but heavy runoffs.

Fifty yards from the line of trees and the unrevealed bank of the arroyo, Matt noticed quick movement off the his right. He stopped the horse and watched. In a moment a coyote, ears held straight up, emerged from the tangled brush and stood immobile, staring at Matt. The coyote yipped once, then turned and ran off in a westerly direction. In a moment another coyote made an appearance, but this one was carrying something.

The second coyote took only peripheral notice of Matt. It was busy trying to make an exit without dropping the object held in its mouth. Matt squinted into the harsh sunlight. Damn, he told himself, that's a bone the critter's carryin'. Matt spurred the buckskin and raced after the fast-moving coyote. It darted into the brush . . . emerged again . . . then darted back in. Matt stayed on open ground, riding parallel to the loping coyote.

It was a big bone . . . a long bone. Big enough and long enough—at least, it appeared so—to be a part of a human skeleton. The bone in the coyote's mouth was not something that Matt could ignore. After so many days of unproductive searching, even the smallest clue dictated investigation. The next time Matt caught sight of the fleeing animal, it no longer had the bone.

Matt pulled up, guided the horse toward the thick growth of mesquite, and took the horse into the brush. He worked his way back upstream, carefully scrutinizing the area between the point where he had last seen the coyote with the bone and the point where he observed that the coyote no longer had the bone. Nothing. He circled back . . . twisted in and out. No bone.

Matt decided to go back to the place where he first had seen the coyote. At that point he moved through the brush and rode along the edge of the four-foot drop-off. After proceeding several hundred yards, he took notice of a small clearing . . . no more than eight or ten feet across.

On the ground and scattered about were other bones . . . a portion of spine with ribs attached . . . small bones here and there. A strange feeling ran through Matt's body. His stomach tightened. He rode forward into the clearing.

A long bone, lying near the gnarled trunk of an old mesquite, caught his eye. Like the bone carried by the coyote, it might be . . . It might be what? He asked himself. He rode closer . . . stopped and examined the bone. He couldn't tell. A leg bone . . . an arm bone. He couldn't tell. He turned the horse slowly. His eyes caught sight of another similar bone.

This time Matt dismounted, pushed aside some limbs, and approached the bone. It was lying in a patch of thick, dead grass. Matt touched the object with the toe of his boot . . . moved it a little. As he did, he saw the small pointed hoof attached.

Matt took a deep breath and let it out slowly. Only the remains of a desert deer . . . killed perhaps by a cougar . . . the bones left for the wandering coyotes. Matt mounted up again and went down the bank of the wash, crossing it to the east.

As Matt rode, he wondered what his swirling feelings were trying to tell him. Was he glad that the bones weren't the bones of a man? The bones of his friend, Cleve Madison? Of course! Yet, he told himself, if Cleve's remains were discovered, that would be the end of all the consternation and not knowing . . . of the nagging fears and worry. Then life could return to normal on the Madison ranch. But in Matt, as in most human beings, hope was the last thing to leave, and since the bones had been only animal bones, Matt still had hope. Not much, but a little something to cling to. As long as he had that, he would continue the search.

Matt turned and looked over his shoulder and into the pale sky, noting the position of the sun. Four hours of light, maybe a little more. Good, Matt told himself. He should arrive in Tubac just a little before darkness settled in.

Matt was moving out of the flat grassland and up into rolling desert hill country . . . dry, rocky, supporting a sparse growth of greasewood and stands of spiny cholla. For an instant Matt's mind recalled Alicia as she had turned and ridden away from him back at the point of rocks. Burdened even with her troubles, her back had been ramrod straight . . . shoulders thrown back . . . chin high. And the hair . . . the long, sun-bleached hair . . . some of it fanning across her back . . . some of it falling forward of her shoulders and lying across the contours of her breasts remained vivid in Matt's memory. He was aware that he was compiling a lengthening list of mental images of the alluring Alicia. Not surprising, he told himself. He had a most distinct feeling that she would have a similar effect on nearly any man breathing and with a few drops of blood running in his veins.

What if? Matt couldn't surpress the bothersome conjecturing. What if Cleve never returns? What if we find his remains eventually . . . or confirm in some manner that he will never be returning? Matt asked himself. At least, not returning as a living, breathing husband to Alicia. Matt felt almost sure that Alicia would ask him to stay on. Then what? Like many questions, it was ponderable but not answerable. He smiled a tiny smile . . . knowing that he had been smitten by Alicia and her stunning desert transformation. But, he told himself, she wasn't his and couldn't be his. She was the wife of his very best friend. So be it, he told himself . . . not ashamed of his momentary fantasy . . . knowing beyond doubt that he would never attempt to move his fantasy into the realm of reality. According to Matt Ramsey's personal set of standards, that would be something as forbidden as the fruit in the ancient garden.

After another hour of riding at a smooth and comfortable pace, Matt topped out on a high plateau that looked out on the valley of the Santa Cruz. In the far distance he could see a speck that he knew to be the crumbling and unfinished bell tower of old Tumacacori. And not far away, in another direction he could see the white walls of the once bustling presidio of Tubac.

The sun was gone . . . an hour nearly behind the towering bulk of the Baboquivaris. Dusk had fallen across the land. He continued on, and shortly before the surrounding desert would be plunged into total darkness, Matt turned his horse into the wagon tracks that led to Riggs's store.

This time it was not necessary for him to read the instructions tacked next to the heavy gate. He knew what to do. He clanged the bell and waited. It was a longer wait this time, and just as Matt was prepared to ring again . . . the deep, gravelly voice boomed out, "Who's there?"

"Matt Ramsey . . . visited here a few days back."

"So you did, Matt," Riggs's voice replied. "Well, come on in."

Although Riggs gave him no further instructions, Matt unstrapped his gunbelt and held it above his head as he opened the gate and edged through. He took a few steps and stopped by the opened gun box that stood beside the walkway. He heard the grating laugh from behind the barred shutters. "No need to stash your weapon . . . come on in."

The dark-feathered hawk perched silently on a rocky shelf that hung above the rapidly darkening canyon. A canyon high in the mountains called the Baboquivaris.

The canyon below the hawk was a very deep and precipitous canyon. Narrow . . . in many places less that eight feet wide; yet, its sides—sheer rock—rose in jagged and perpendicular height for more than a hundred and fifty feet. Not a sprig or a sprout grew along the face of the canyon wall, and its bed was composed solely of tumbled rock. Formed by endless eons of rushing water, the canyon was one of a countless number of such small side canyons that joined with larger canyons in the tossed interior of the wilderness mountains.

Long before the hawk had landed on its cliffside perch, two riders had entered the canyon and proceeded with considerable difficulty to the point where its boxed end prevented further passage.

The hawk, taking brief surcease after a day of hunting, scarcely turned its head when the hollow roar of a firearm raced like a thunderbolt down the canyon. The same held true when a second report followed quickly on the heels of the first.

In a few minutes the clatter of hooves against raw stone made a dim audible impression on the sharp-eyed bird. But these were not the types of sounds that meant anything to the hawk. If the sounds had been those of a small mouse, that would have been an entirely different matter.

The hawk did not even glance down at the movement below. Took no note at all of the dark-robed figure guiding a single horse down the narrow canyon . . . retracing steps that had earlier been taken by two horses and two men.

# CHAPTER

# ★ 10 ★

Riggs fed Matt from a pot of stew . . . gave some to his black cat, too. "I et early," Riggs told him. "Worked my ass off today." Then he laughed. "Cut about six or eight pieces of wood and carried a little water for my plants. Tough life, ain't it?"

Matt smiled. He liked Riggs . . . a tough old man who had seen much in his lifetime. After Matt and the cat had finished their stew, Riggs invited him to move to the sitting area in front of a fireplace with a rock mantel. Even though summer was approaching, the desert cooled rapidly after the end of day and Riggs had a small fire in the fireplace. "I like a fire," he told Matt. "Like lookin' into the glowin' coals. Puts a man at ease, I believe. But summer's comin' on, and it won't be tolerable to have a fire much longer."

"I like a fire, too," Matt told him as he took a seat in a leather-backed chair a few feet from the small fire.

Riggs disappeared for a few moments. Since it wasn't actually cold enough for a fire, Riggs had thrown back the heavy plank shutters on two large windows in the front of the house. Matt took note of the fact that both of these windows had heavy iron bars securely in place. He also noted that the chairs were placed so they were shielded from the open windows by thick adobe walls. Old man Riggs took no chances. That, of course, was why he had endured when so many had not on the harsh and unforgiving frontier of Arizona.

Riggs returned with a pair of cups . . . handed one to Matt. "Little whiskey goes good with a nice fire at the end of a day. I trust you agree?"

"Surely do," Matt replied. As they sat in the quiet of the desert evening, Matt told the old man about the disappearance of Cleve Madison . . . about the endless searching and the absence of any clues. Finished, he asked the logical question. "You got any ideas?"

Riggs sat for a long time . . . stroked his scraggly beard and considered it. After a considerable passage of time Matt spoke. "I came over to see you because I thought just maybe he might have been here." Still silence. Riggs was weighing it all.

Finally Riggs shook his head from side to side. "Naw. Ain't been here. Guess I haven't seen Cleve Madison in nearly two months. See Pete Waggoner damn near every weekend, but as I told you before, he ain't been by recently. Now I know why . . . out lookin' for his boss."

"Who has stopped by here lately? Especially a couple of weeks back. Anybody?"

Riggs smiled. "Well, when you live out here alone as I do, you can pretty well remember everyone who stops in. Some cowboys from over east of the Santa Ritas come in a few days before you did. And one prospector about a week before you showed up. Since you showed up, I've had two more prospectors and a man named Ruggles who was comin' up from Mexico with a pretty but plump Mexican bride. That's it."

Matt leaned forward and rested his elbows on his knees. "You got any thoughts on this whole matter?"

Riggs squinched up his face. "Could be one of several things. I wouldn't suggest one to be any more likely than another."

"Any chance he just pulled out and left it all . . . for some kind of reason?"

"No reason . . . not for him. He loved this country . . . loved his wife . . . was makin' out good with his cattle."

"He was in the war," Matt said. "We marched and fought together. Saw some bad killin' . . . did some ourselves. I've heard tell that experiences like that sometimes affect a man's mind. I haven't seen Cleve in a good many years . . . have no basis for makin' a judgment on somethin' like that."

Riggs shook his head in the negative, "Naw . . . not him. Nothin' wrong with his head." They sat for a while, rocking and sipping at the whiskey. As the evening wore on. Matt told him about Alicia . . . the shocking transformation that he had observed.

Riggs smiled as Matt talked . . . nodded his head in agreement. "I seen her when they was comin' down here the first time. She was in here . . . made the air about twice as heavy as it usually is. I watched the change . . . like the change of seasons . . . noticin' a little change every time I seen her. She's a good woman . . . a strong woman. She'll hold up. I can tell the type. With or without Cleve she'll ranch the land and live on it for all the rest of her years. She's become a part of the land . . . a part of the territory."

The fire burned down into only a small mound of coals. Riggs went off and refilled their whiskey cups. When he returned, Matt told him of the sudden leaving of Alicia's Indian workers and of the black-robed priest and his quest for the lost mission. He also mentioned the story that the Mexican cowboy José had told him about the chain of missions and the mines in which the Indians were forced to labor.

At the end of it Riggs chuckled. "Nothin' like a gold story to get a man's interest. You thinkin' about a trek into the Baboquivaris?"

"Not hardly," Matt said, smiling. "I had my attack of gold fever up in Colorado. Doubt that I would walk over even one hill to look for lost treasure or a lost mine."

"You never know," said Riggs. "But stories do circulate about the Baboquivaris. Have you ever noticed," he asked, "that all the really rich lost mines or all the really big treasures are always in some god-awful country that can hardly be penetrated by man? The worse the country, the bigger the prize. They say that a lost mine is an imaginary hole with a liar standin' at the top." Riggs wheezed and cackled at his own statement. Probably startin' to feel the whiskey, Matt conjectured.

"Well, tell me," said Matt, "what kind of stories do they tell about the Baboquivaris?"

Riggs laughed again. "Damn near any kind of story you want to hear. But some are repeated more than others. Don't know that makes 'em true. It's just that the best ones get told most. For example . . ." Riggs took a long swig of the liquor.

Matt slouched low in the chair, feeling warm and relaxed . . . waiting for the story to begin.

Riggs wiped at his mouth, smacked his lips a few times, and started. "Seems that a good many people believe that there was a mission somewhere back in the Baboquivaris . . . heard that many times myself. José was right what he told you about some of the Jesuits goin' bad and puttin' the poor ignorant Indians to work. Tried to scare 'em into it by tellin' horrible stories of hell and damnation if they didn't bring the Lord's gold and silver out of the ground. If that didn't work, they let the Spanish soldiers convince 'em with whips.

"Supposedly, there was a whole chain of missions stretchin' east to west from California and then another chain from down in Mexico and up to our part of the country. We got one of 'em right up the road a piece, Tumacacori. Now, the story as I got it is that the gold and silver—and there was supposed to have been god-awful amounts of it—was eventually transported east of here to a point on the San Pedro River. From there it was taken on to some other place . . . damned if I know where . . . most likely a seaport on the Gulf of Mexico. Then shipped to Spain."

Matt cut in. "How long did all of this go on?"

"A long time, I'm told. Couple of centuries. You can mine a lot of gold in a couple of centuries. Anyhow, they needed a safe place along the general line of missions to use as a storage stop. So they built a small mission way back in the Baboquivaris that served the main purpose of holdin' gold and silver bullion as it was moved along the route. Can't recall the name of the mission."

"San Acacia del Norte. I think that's what the priest called it."

Riggs nodded. "That's it. Well, anyway . . . that's what they say. They say there's a lot of gold up there. Maybe it's already been found. Maybe just found and not taken out . . . maybe found and hauled off. A good many years back, before the War Between the States, when Tubac here was a bustlin' community, three foreigners was supposed to have arrived here. As I've heard it told, some say they was Frenchmen and others say they was Germans. Anyhow, they spoke bad English and had accents. They asked a lot of questions and bought a lot of supplies, then took off toward the west.

"After a period of time they returned. They bought more supplies. Bought 'em this time with raw gold. It was said that the gold was in the form of shavin's . . . like it had been carved off of gold ingots. At any rate, not plain old nuggets like prospectors wash out of a creek. They also bought themselves a lot of likker and had a whoppin' good time durin' their stay. Then they took off again. This comin' and goin' kept up for a good many months.

"Finally a tough and enterprisin' Mexican man—his name was Proculo, they say—decided to follow them into the mountains. Proculo was known as a brawler and trouble-maker . . . hell-raiser, you might say. Anyhow, as it's told, Proculo dogged their trail all the way into the Baboquivaris and through the canyons, supposedly to the place where they were getting the loot. But he was discovered and captured."

The cat appeared from a dark corner of the room and began rubbing itself against Matt's leg. "Did they kill him?" Matt asked.

"Well, that was probably their intention. But it appears that their main intention was to send a warnin'. They tied Proculo down, then one of 'em—one of the foreigners— took a hammer and a pair of forty-penny nails—them big suckers—and nailed them nails up through Proculo's jaw on both sides. Nailed his mouth plumb shut. That's a strong message . . . a message that said we don't intend for this man to tell about anything he saw. Then they hauled him out of the mountain and hung him by his wrists to a tree near the edge of the Altar Valley. I'm sure they expected him to die, but he didn't, and he was rescued by a passing wagon carryin' supplies to the south.

"Well, Proculo bein' a tough hombre got took up to the pueblo of Tucson, where a doctor and a blacksmith, workin' together, got them nails out of his jaws. It took a long time healin', and I suppose durin' that time Proculo did a lot of angry thinkin'.

"Eventually, Proculo slipped back down to Tubac with a brace of wicked-lookin' pistols and a rifle and waited. He followed the foreigners out again . . . this time bein' somewhat more cautious.

"A few people in Tubac knew what was goin' on, so they waited expectantly. Who would return, Proculo or the foreigners? Many months passed. And the end of the story is that none of 'em ever returned. So . . . what happened? Some say Proculo bushwhacked 'em after bein' led to the treasure, and he made off with a vast amount of gold . . . headin' somewhere else . . . back down to Mexico maybe or on to California. Some say the foreigners bushwhacked Proculo and decided it would be a poor idea to keep comin' back to Tubac. Anyway, that's the story."

"It's a good story," Matt told him. "So apparently there is some reason to believe that a lost mission is up in those mountains."

"Probably," Riggs replied.

"Funny thing," said Matt. "That priest told us all about the mission . . . gave us lots of details and information . . . practically described it for us. Yet, he never mentioned gold. Never said a word about gold or silver or any kind of treasure."

"He didn't say, by any chance, that his name was Father Proculo, did he?" Then Riggs rocked back in his chair and laughed loudly. Matt smiled in return. It was pleasant sitting in Riggs's thick-walled house and spinning stories. For the first time since he found out about Cleve's disappearance, Matt Ramsey felt relaxed. The whiskey, he surmised, had something to do with it.

# CHAPTER

## ★ 11 ★

Shortly after Riggs's rooster greeted the new day, Matt departed Tubac and worked his way north to a shallow pass that took him to the west of the Sierrita Mountains and then across Big Brawley Wash, a sandy conduit that seemed to Matt to be even wider than the Santa Cruz. This was McNeal country, a wide basin that appeared every bit as good for cattle as the land on Cleve's Circle M.

Riggs had told Matt to ride about ten miles west of Brawley and look for some low hills just north of west. Matt located the hills about midday and had no trouble discerning the big rock house on the top of one of them. As he approached, one of McNeal's cowhands rode out to greet him . . . introduced himself as Fred Ganung. "Yes, indeed," Fred told Matt, "Mr. McNeal is at the house and will surely enjoy a visit with a man from Texas."

They sat on the wide porch overlooking the valley, seated in rocking chairs . . . McNeal with his feet up on the porch railing.

Alicia had told Matt that McNeal was from back East, and the man's accent confirmed it. On top of that the cattleman told Matt that he was from Boston, chuckling as he did so. "Not very good credentials for taming the Arizona frontier, but I'm learning. Actually, I'm a partner in this enterprise. It was decided that one of us should come out and run the place. Since I had no wife or kids at home—my wife died some years back—they convinced me to be the one. Glad I did it," he concluded.

Later Matt told McNeal that Alicia appreciated the help he was offering in the search for her missing husband. McNeal looked troubled when the talk turned to Cleve. He wrinkled his brow and shook his head slowly. "It's a damn puzzle," he told Matt. "Up this way we've covered near two hundred square miles . . . covered them the best we could. Two of my men are out today."

As the conversation progressed, Matt began to hold the impression that McNeal was not as ugly a man as he appeared to Alicia. Of course, a slick rat can do that, he told himself: pretend to be whatever he wants to be if it serves his purpose.

After a bit it was McNeal, himself, who mentioned the nature of his relationship with Alicia. "I know she doesn't care much for me. Had a little run-in with Cleve some months back . . . seven or eight, I guess. I pushed him a little too hard, said some things I probably shouldn't have. But bear in mind, I'm new to ranching. Guess I saw an opportunity to earn some money for the partnership—maybe a whole lot of money—and I bore down on him. I guess ahead of everything else I'm a businessman, and sometimes business gets in the way of relationships."

Matt decided to seize the opportunity and hit McNeal with a straightforward question. "That misunderstanding wouldn't have been over some land you wanted to lease, would it?"

McNeal didn't hesitate. "Yes, it was."

Matt got straightforward again. "For what purpose were you wanting to lease that land, Mr. McNeal?"

McNeal looked Matt straight in the eye. "Probably you know that I didn't tell him why. In looking back, it was a mistake. I should have told him." McNeal paused for a moment, then asked a question. "You ever get involved with gold . . . mining gold, looking for gold?"

Matt smiled. "Yep . . . I had two years of it up in Colorado. Never made a dime. I'm cured."

"Perhaps you know, then, that the prospect of large amounts of gold can affect a man's thinking."

"I do," said Matt.

"That's what happened to me," McNeal told him. "About seven or eight months back a Mexican representing a wealthy rancher below the border—a rancher who remained unnamed—came to the ranch and offered me a business proposition. He told me that he had tried unsuccessfully to lease some of Madison's land . . . a long strip that runs through the foothills of the Baboquivaris. He asked me to try to effect the lease myself, and then, if I was successful, to give the wealthy Mexican rancher access to the land. That was all he wanted, and he offered me a very impressive fee if I could pull it off."

"And you decided to give it a try?"

"Not immediately," McNeal replied. "I invited the Mexican to stay over a few days while I thought on it. I couldn't figure why the rancher in Mexico would be willing to pay Madison a good price to lease it and additionally offer me a big fee for arranging it. So . . . I asked him. And what he told me, I figured was pure bullshit, as they say. He said that this rich rancher owed a debt of gratitude to the order of Jesuit priests. Said that the rancher believed that the Jesuits, through their prayers, had miraculously saved a close relative from a serious illness. He wanted to help them locate an old abandoned mission that they had been seeking for many years. It didn't add up."

The cook stepped out on the porch and announced lunch for McNeal and his guest. They moved from porch to dining room, and over food, McNeal continued. "I'm a well-read man . . . a graduate of Harvard. That doesn't necessarily make me brilliant, but it does make me well-read. I know the history of the Spanish missions, the mining and hoarding of gold. So I came right out and told my visitor that I suspected that they were looking for gold. He didn't confirm that they were, but after a lot of beating around the bush, he finally said that on top of the fee I would get a share of any profit from any business enterprise associated with the leased land. When he said that, I knew I was right. I felt strongly that it was hoarded Spanish treasure they were after."

The cook appeared and removed their plates . . . returned almost immediately with slices of fresh apple pie. Matt was curious. "But this man never mentioned the name of his superior . . . the rancher who sent him?"

"No," replied McNeal, "and I didn't press it. By this time the gold was dancing in my eyes. I was thinking big, as I usually do . . . thinking millions and also thinking how impressed my partners would be if I brought that kind of money in on top of the cattle profits. So I bore in hard on Cleve Madison, but he had no desire to lease land to me or anyone else. I pushed too hard, and now, especially with his disappearance, I'm sorry I did."

McNeal looked up at Matt. Matt's eyes were boring into the man from the east, but McNeal held fast and didn't avert his look . . . even as Matt asked his question. "Did you intend to split this treasure money with Cleve?"

"I knew you would eventually ask that question. I did, but, knowing Cleve Madison, I wanted to get the deal set first, then let him in on it. You have every right to doubt my word if you so desire."

Matt *did* doubt his word. Surely, Matt told himself, if McNeal was the businessman he claimed to be, he would have realized the value of letting Cleve know of the possibility of lost gold and the opportunity to make some big and easy money. Matt had known Cleve Madison under all kinds of conditions . . . from the best to the most difficult. Cleve knew the value of money and what it would buy, and he, most likely, would have been a willing partner in a venture to unearth lost Spanish gold. Now Matt was beginning to see why Alicia was less than fond of McNeal. McNeal had a streak of greed and possibly other defects of character that hadn't surfaced yet. But Matt was pretty sure that those defects did not include the ability to kill a neighbor for potential profit of any kind.

"At any rate," said McNeal, "my men will continue searching, but after so long a period of time, I hold out small hope that Cleve will be found."

Matt sat quietly for a few moments. One thing he hadn't mentioned to McNeal was the visit from the priest or the priest's trek into the Baboquivaris to search for the mission. Was the earlier visit by the Mexican emissary tied somehow to the more recent arrival of the wandering Jesuit? A good question, Matt told himself, but not one he would discuss with McNeal.

"Care to stay over?" asked McNeal.

"Thanks," said Matt, "but I'm expected back."

"Well, in that case, I'll ride south with you a distance." McNeal placed his napkin on the table and got to his feet. Matt did likewise, paused at the kitchen door to call his compliments to the cowboy cook, and followed McNeal out into the bright Arizona sunlight.

They rode slowly, chatting mostly about the land, grazing conditions, and life in general on the frontier. Matt had one question on his mind, and he finally asked it. "Tell me," he inquired, "why would it be necessary to go into the Baboquivaris through Circle M land? Why not go in from another point . . . maybe from the western side of the range?"

McNeal reined his horse and pointed toward the southwest. "They could go around to the western side, but that would mean an extra seventy to a hundred miles each way. On top of that, the western side is even more rugged than this side . . . lots of sheer rock faces. Really bad country." McNeal pointed again. "That tallest point is Baboquivari Peak. Just to the north and directly west of Madison's place, you can see that the general slope of the range is a gentler rise. Of course, I'm speaking in relative terms. Above the foothills, none of that country is fit for a wagon road, but the area just north of the peak is the best way in. Logically, I would imagine that if there was a mission up there, it would be reached through the country I just pointed out."

A nagging question was bothering Matt. Maybe McNeal had an answer. "Somethin' I'm curious about," said Matt. "It seems that building a mission would require that lots of equipment and heavy stuff would have to be taken to the site . . . like a large bell, maybe. I've heard that some of those church bells are mighty big . . . mighty heavy. How would they get something like that in there without a wagon road?"

"How did they move the huge stones that went into the building of the ancient pyramids?" asked McNeal. Then he answered his own question. "They did it with human labor . . . slave labor. Earlier years here in the southwest under the heel of Spanish conquest were not good years for the natives. If an object—a bell, say—weighed five hundred pounds . . . a thousand . . . whatever . . . it could be lashed between heavy beams, then carried on the shoulders of enslaved Indians. If one dropped, he could be replaced. I assume it was as simple as that."

Matt rode silently for a few moments, then spoke. "It's little wonder then that the Indians so resent the comin' of the white man."

"The Apache, of course, are different from many of the tribes. They, as far as I know, have never carried anything for a white man. I've lost three cowboys to Apache. All found with their scalps missing. Keep an eye out when you ride."

After proceeding slightly more than five miles to the south, the two of them reached a water tank with a single large cottonwood tree growing at its edge. They stopped in the shade and watered the horses. McNeal offered his hand and Matt shook it. "I'll be heading back now," McNeal said. "Please give my regards to Alicia and tell her that we are still sending men out to search."

"I'll do that," Matt replied. "Thanks much for the good lunch." He touched the tip of his hat. "See you again, I'm sure." Then he reined his horse and rode on toward the south.

As he rode, Matt continued his thinking. Maybe it wasn't so strange after all, he told himself, the coincidence—or apparent coincidence—between the Mexican rancher wanting to help the Jesuits and the more recent arrival of Father Arredondo. In fact, it even made sense . . . or so it seemed. The Jesuits hoping to find a lost mission . . . a grateful and wealthy rancher stepping in to help to no avail . . . and later the church sends one of its priests out on a quest that probably had been planned before the Mexican rancher ever became involved.

But as Matt rode, he cranked in the business about lost gold. José, Riggs, and McNeal had all mentioned lost gold in the Baboquivaris. Gold makes men do strange things, often bad things, Matt reminded himself. Could there possibly be a connection between the lost gold of the Baboquivaris and Cleve's disappearance? It didn't seem so . . . but nevertheless . . .

He wondered who the nameless and wealthy Mexican rancher might be. Even though he lived somewhere below the border, Alicia might know of such a man. He would ask her upon his return.

# CHAPTER

# ★12★

Matt arrived back at the Circle M Ranch in darkness. Juanita had warm food waiting for him, and Alicia was anxious to hear of his journey to Tubac and and the swing by McNeal's ranch. They sat in the cool of the evening on the wide front porch and talked. Yet, as usual, there was nothing concrete to discuss. Alicia, like Matt, had come across no real evidence during the two-day period.

"One thing I feel sure of," said Matt, "is that Cleve did not purposely or voluntarily leave this part of the country. Riggs, like you, felt that Cleve was very sound of mind and very happy with you and the ranch. I think that's one possibility that we can toss aside and forget."

"The hurt is really starting to settle in," she replied. "A part of me is beginning to accept it. But what I can't seem to handle is just giving up and returning to what you would call a normal routine. How can a person do something like that?"

Matt sat quietly, unable to come up with a suitable answer. Instead, he queried her about the wealthy Mexican rancher to the south. "You know any of the people down that way?"

"No," she replied. "People don't pass back and forth across the border very much. Neither Cleve nor I have ever been down into Mexico. We've been kept too busy with the ranch to do any traveling of that sort."

"How about this emissary that the wealthy rancher sent up here? Of course, we don't know that he was actually representing any wealthy rancher . . . but tell me about him."

"A pleasant man who spoke rather broken English. I wasn't in on the conversation about leasing the land, but Cleve told me that the man wanted to arrange for a lease . . . for five years. Money wasn't the problem. The offer was fair. Cleve simply wasn't inclined to lease land to strangers for a reason that the man didn't care to explain."

"Did you know," asked Matt, "why McNeal sometime later wanted to lease the same strip of land?"

"No."

"McNeal told me that a man representing the same Mexican rancher approached him. Asked McNeal to lease the land. Afterward, the Mexican rancher, for a large fee paid to McNeal, would take over the land."

Alicia bristled. "That sounds like McNeal. Willing to do anything to make money."

But Matt asked for her patience and went on to tell her about McNeal's belief that the Mexican wanted the land so that wealthy rancher could search for the lost gold of the mission of San Acacia del Norte. "Tell me what you think," Matt suggested. "Both your cowboys, José and Riggs, have heard stories about a lot of buried gold at the old mission in the Baboquivaris, and McNeal feels that the reason the Mexicans wanted the land was to search for the lost treasure. Consider this. A wealthy Mexican rancher is itchin' for the gold he believes is in those mountains. Cleve disappears. Now a priest is up there tryin' to find the old mission. My question is this. Does your mind tend to tie those three things together?"

Alicia's answer was a long time in coming. "I can see the wealthy Mexican wanting more wealth, but it would do him no good to kill Cleve. That would accomplish nothing. As for the priest . . . surely a priest, a man of God, wouldn't be a part of a plot that would call for the murder of my husband. Do you think otherwise?"

Matt sighed. "I don't know. Since we've got no real clues . . . only these scraps . . . a wealthy Mexican . . . a wanderin' priest . . . I guess you tend to work over the scraps. Like a pup that chews at a bone with nothin' on it."

Alicia stood up. "I'm terribly tired, Matt. I'm going to get some sleep. It's not work that's doing it . . . it's the worry. Can you stay with us for a while?"

"As long as you need me."

"I was thinking," she said, "of going out tomorrow to a deep gulley this side of the Las Guijas Mountains . . . not far off the route you took to Tubac. Remember the dead calf we saw some days back . . . killed by a cougar?" Matt nodded. "Now you've told me about a killed deer over in the same area. Cleve said for some time that he thought a couple of lions might be working out of the canyon near the Las Guijas. I'd like to go over there."

Matt spoke softly. "A lion didn't get Cleve. Regardless of all the stories you hear, mountain lions don't attack healthy humans ridin' horses."

"I know that," said Alicia. "But Cleve might have decided to go in there hunting them. We *have* lost several head of young stock lately. If he had an accident, it could have been in there. It's an area we haven't searched yet."

"Good enough," Matt replied.

The next day Matt and Alicia scoured the countryside to the north and west of the small Las Guijas range but saw nothing of cougars or Cleve. The following day the two of them traveled toward the northeast and found nothing.

As usual, they stayed away the entire day, returning near dusk. When they rode up to the ranch house, the foreman, Pete Waggoner, and Father Arredondo were standing on the steps of the porch.

"Howdy," said Alicia, smiling. "Back from the mountains, eh?"

"We've got a problem," said Pete. "Young Bob didn't come in with the Father."

Alicia and Matt got down from their horses. "Didn't come back?" queried Alicia.

The priest stepped down from the porch. "Perhaps this is my fault. We were two days into the mountains. I had pushed on ahead after finding an old, rusted mule shoe. In my fervor I failed to look back. When I finally stopped and did so, the young man was not behind me. I retraced my path, but we had been in a maze of twisting canyons. I, myself, became confused."

"This happened day before yesterday?" Matt inquired.

"*Sí.* Finally I found the main canyon, the one we had originally been following. I waited there . . . called many times. I made camp . . . kept a good fire going through the night, thinking perhaps he would see it. But the next day I assumed that he had decided to return to the ranch. I continued on, but it finally occurred to me that if he returned, he might report *me* as being lost. Then you would all leave your work and come looking for me. It seemed wise for me to return—as I have—and now I find that the boy did not come back."

"You think we should get a search party ready and head out?" asked Pete.

Matt looked to Alicia. He thought he saw her body sway just a little . . . her knees start to buckle. She leaned her head against the horse for a moment . . . seemed to recover her composure. "He's all right," she finally said. "Bob is all right. This is not the same as Cleve's disappearance."

Matt felt that Alicia was believing what she wanted to believe. He was sure that she had nearly fainted with the news. The pressure on Alicia was sizable, no doubt about that. "He could be lookin' for the padre," Matt suggested.

"That's what I'm thinking," said Alicia. "I gave him orders to keep a close eye on you, Father. He's a very responsible young man." She went and sat on the edge of the porch. "Bob knows the outdoors. He could survive in any of this country indefinitely on his own." She looked at the priest. "Tell me where you were . . . what part of the mountains."

"I have some very old maps . . . from the church archives . . . and we were going in the direction suggested by one of the maps. Heading north beyond the tallest peak, up a huge canyon. We had climbed to within perhaps two thousand feet of the summit . . . not the peak itself, but the general ridge that runs north." He paused, apparently trying to gather his thoughts.

"Here's what I'm guessing," said Alicia. "Bob would have continued on in the direction he believed you were headed. Probably, he would have eventually wound up on the ridge, up in the pine country. If I were in Bob's boots, I would then ride north, scanning the countryside below in an effort to spot you, Father. If I didn't have any luck, I'd come down the mountains through Coyotero Wash . . . a big canyon that empties into the Altar Valley farther north." She paused for a moment, took a deep breath. "I don't want us losing our heads over this. All of us have been under a lot of pressure over Cleve's disappearance. We need to stay calm."

Pete cut in. "If he's done what you think he'd do, then he'd be in the vicinity of McNeal's place when he comes out of the mountains. How about me and Manuel ridin' up that way tomorrow and checkin' things out?" Pete tried to smile. "Hell, he might be chewin' on one of McNeal's juicy beefsteaks at this very moment."

"That's fine," said Alicia.

"And I," said the priest, "will leave before light tomorrow morning. I will attempt to go back over the route we traveled previously. I feel a responsibility."

"I want someone to go with you." She turned to Matt. "Will you go with him?"

"If you want," said Matt.

"No, no," interjected Father Arredondo. "You have done too much already, and I don't want to be responsible for anyone else going with me into that fearsome country. Especially you, Señor Ramsey. You are not familiar with those devil mountains."

Alicia considered the priest's remarks. "Let me think on it," she said. "This is all happening too fast. I need a little time to myself."

Pete Waggoner spoke up. "Me and the padre was on our way to the corral to take a look at his horse . . . loose shoe, he thinks."

"Go ahead," Alicia told them. After they left, she sat for a long time, chewing gently on her upper lip. Finally she looked at Matt. He was looking at her. Neither of them spoke right away. She stood up. "I want you to go with him."

"He said he don't want me. I'm not anxious to go where I'm not wanted."

"Then follow him," she said. "Just keep track of him. I'm really having a very difficult time with all of this. If someone else disappears, I don't know . . ." Her voice trailed off.

Matt thought on it for a while. "I guess I could. Hope I can. The padre seems like a seasoned traveler . . . a man used to workin' his way through rough country. But probably I can keep up with him . . . keep him in sight." Then he asked a question. "You really feel Bob is all right?"

"I have to believe it," she replied.

"I'll follow him," Matt said. "Let's go have some supper. I want Juanita to pull together some grub for me. I'll take the food and my bedroll down to the outbuilding by the corral and leave it there. No need to rile the padre. When he said he didn't want anyone along, he meant it."

Late that night Matt, in his sock feet, paced in his room, then went to the window that faced out on the wide Altar Valley. He leaned into the sill of thick adobe, resting his upper weight on the heavy, plastered blocks of dried mud. Thinking. Earlier today, he told himself, we had Cleve missing, a wealthy rancher with a hunger for lost gold, and a priest lookin' for an old mission. Now . . . we can add another missing man. An owl hooted in the distance. Life takes odd twists, he mused. He had come to the Circle M to relax and visit with old friends. Instead, come the dawn, he would be tracking a black robe into the awesome wilderness of the Baboquivari. That wouldn't do anything to bring his missing friend back. All of a sudden, Matt Ramsey felt useless. Everything, it seemed, was beyond his control. Well, he finally told himself, my food and bedroll are down at the corral, and there isn't one other worthwhile thing I can do this day.

So he blew out the candle and went to bed.

# CHAPTER

## ★ 13 ★

Matt sat in the before-dawn darkness on the far side of the rock and adobe outbuilding, sitting on the ground with his back against his blankets, which he had rolled inside a ground cloth. As he sat, waiting for the priest to take his leave of the Circle M and head back into the Baboquivaris, Matt went through a mental checklist. Rifle, Colt strapped to his waist, food, all the water he could sensibly carry . . . and, of course, the bedroll he was resting against. At Alicia's suggestion he had even included a hip-length jacket. "Nights can get nippy in those upper canyons," she had warned. Well, he told himself, he was as ready as he knew how to be for his unusual assignment, watching over a wandering priest with a stubborn streak and a preference for solitude.

As soon as the first gray light permitted him to define distant objects, Matt heard a door banging at the main house. In a few moments he heard voices, then the soft crunch of approaching feet.

Once they were inside the corral, Matt had no trouble defining the voices. They were the voices he had expected . . . Pete, Alicia, and Father Arredondo. A horse snorted, Pete cajoled it. Alicia spoke. "Please use caution, Father. When should we expect you back?"

"Probably no more than three days, señora. According to

my maps, I was making good progress when I felt the need to turn back. I will retrace old ground and then explore the new. The country is difficult up that way."

"I know it is," replied Alicia.

Next, Matt heard Pete's voice. "Horse is ready, Father."

Sounds carried well on the soft dawn air. Matt could even hear the creak of leather as the priest swung into the saddle. Now the priest's voice carried. "When the young man, Bob, returns, tell him I am sorry to have caused him worry and inconvenience."

"We'll give him one more day to come in," Alicia replied. "If he doesn't show by tomorrow, I'm going to send Pete up to McNeal's. Good chance he'll come back that way."

"Very well, then," said the priest.

Matt listened until the sound of horse's hooves diminished and faded away entirely. Then he rose, picked up his gear, and walked around the building to the corral. Pete and Alicia were waiting for him. Pete had his buckskin saddled.

"You be careful, too," Alicia cautioned.

Matt smiled. "I'm not sure this is a job I relish . . . followin' a man who doesn't want to be followed. If he's like most of them wanderin' missionaries, he's been doin' this for a good many years. Doesn't need me lookin' out for him. I figure it'll be more than embarrassin' if he catches me in the act."

"You tell him I ordered it. That I was concerned for his safety."

"I hope he doesn't see me. That's what I hope."

"If you happen to come across Bob, tell him to come on in and let us know that he's okay."

"That I'll do," said Matt. Finished tying his bedroll on the horse and sliding his rifle into the scabbard, he swung into the saddle and touched the tips of his fingers to the brim of his hat. "See you in a few days." Then he rode out of the corral and headed east toward the dark bulk of mountain whose highest peaks were now touched by early-morning sun.

Matt had no visual sight of the priest for the first mile

or so. I could lose him and never find him, Matt conjectured. But there was nothing he could do about that right now, except take what seemed the easiest and most logical path . . . hoping that that was what the padre had done. Finally, at a high desert ridge that overlooked a wide arroyo, Matt paused and scanned the country ahead. In only a moment he let out a low sigh of relief. The priest was midway across the sandy wash.

Matt watched. When the priest reached and ascended the far bank, he stopped his horse, turned in the saddle, and looked back. That's a little odd, Matt told himself . . . the priest watchin' his back trail. But . . . on second thought . . . maybe not so strange. Ridin' alone and stayin' alive in often grim and hostile country requires a lot of caution. At any rate, Matt told himself, I'll have to stay a little sneaky myself.

Matt stayed in the tangle of greasewood brush until the priest had climbed his horse about halfway up the far ridge. Then Matt started down. He moved slowly, endeavoring, as much as possible, to keep a concealing wall of growth between himself and the missionary. Matt did not put his horse into the wash and cross until the priest had topped out and gone over the ridge. Then, with as much speed as possible in the rough country, Matt went up the incline on the path that the priest had taken.

Just as a test, since he might need it later, Matt watched the ground . . . trying to spot the trail left by the priest's mount. Not too difficult, Matt told himself. The ground, for the most part, was hard-packed sandy loam over even harder caliche. But nearly all the ground was heavily strewn with loose rock. Matt had little trouble locating the places where the horse's hooves had disturbed and tossed the rock. Matt smiled; it would be a different matter when they got into the really bad country. He raised his eyes. Up there in deep and narrow canyons that were almost entirely composed of rock shelves and tossed boulders, tracking would become almost impossible. Then he would have to maintain almost constant visual contact.

In the corrugated country that alternated between high ridges and deep arroyos, Matt followed his strategic pattern.

He would wait in cover at the top of a ridge. Wait until the priest had gone over the ridge ahead . . . then urge his horse down the slope, up the incline . . . then, again, wait at the top of the ridge.

By the time the sun had made its daily appearance, the priest had reached the foothills of the Baboquivari. Now Matt's strategy required a change. The ridges now ran in an easterly direction, angling down from the mountains and out into the lower country. So Matt stayed one ridge to the south of the priest as he climbed his horse higher and higher into the Baboquivaris. The foothills were heavy with brushy palo verde trees and greasewood, so it was not difficult for Matt to maintain concealment.

By midmorning they were into the mountains proper. The priest took the route just north of towering Baboquivari Peak . . . the best route of a bad lot. For the most part the yawning canyon they were following dictated the path. Matt sometimes lost sight of the padre for long periods of time, but eventually he would pick him up again.

Finally they entered country where deep side canyons fed into the main canyon. Now the incline on each side of the primary canyon was extremely steep . . . sometimes a thousand feet or more. The side canyons often had sheer cliffs on either side. Matt, for a time, was concerned that the priest might enter a side-canyon while out of his line of sight. But he quickly dismissed that possibility. No group of people, he told himself, would ever have traversed such rough country to seek a mission site. Besides, not a one of the side-canyons would ever widen into the broad stretch of open ground required for the construction of a large building.

Matt was not an experienced tracker of men. He simply hadn't had frequent cause to trail people, but he was reasonably satisfied with his impromptu tactics. About noon he eased around a bend in the canyon and poked his head out from behind a vertical column of rock. The priest, about a quarter of a mile ahead, was off his horse and seated on a large rock. Matt watched. It appeared the priest was eating. Not a bad idea, Matt told himself. He slipped back to the place where the buckskin was standing, fished in the saddlebag, and took out a parcel of Alicia's fare.

He seated himself back in the deep shadows of a rocky shelf, a place where he could watch the priest, and chewed at thin strips of beef wrapped in soft tortillas, then slaked his thirst with water from one of the leather flasks. When the priest rose from the flat rock, so did Matt.

Shortly after resuming the climb into the mountains, the canyon widened . . . the slopes flattened out just a little . . . and growth appeared along their course. Now the country was sprinkled with the deep green foliage of scattered junipers. In the gullies heavy stands of brush oak followed the twisting but dry streambeds. Thick, low-growing chaparral was scattered along the ridges.

Although the land was more hospitable than in the shadowed canyon, it was still rough country . . . broken by jagged outcroppings of rock and ancient upheavals of the land. At one point Matt lost sight of the priest for better than half an hour. He pushed his horse hard . . . seeking high ground that would provide a better view of the surrounding country. Finally he caught sight of him . . . riding at the bottom of a gully in amongst the heavy stands of scrub oak.

Matt had actually gained on the priest to the extent that he was as far up the mountain as the wandering missionary. His position gave Matt an opportunity to rest the horse, so he sat quietly . . . took a drink. The priest stopped, too . . . reached into his saddlebag and drew forth what Matt assumed was a rolled map. The priest appeared to be studying both the map and the ground ahead. After a few moments he placed the map back in the saddlebag. He altered his direction drastically . . . turning nearly ninety degrees to his left . . . going over a small ridge and disappearing.

Matt decided to give the priest a little more distance, so he continued to sit. The silence of the canyon was intense. Once a bird called, but other than that and the breathing of the horse, the awesome interior of the Baboquivari was as still as a tomb. But suddenly the silence was broken by the distant sound of rock being dislodged. A deer, thought

Matt. He let his eyes carefully scan the land in an uphill direction. He listened, but the sound did not repeat itself.

He couldn't be sure of the place from which the sound came, but he thought it was near a line of cliffs that jutted out on the ridge that had just been crossed by the priest.

Matt watched, waited . . . listened. Then, for a fleeting instant, he sensed movement near the top of the cliffs. He concentrated on that particular area. Then, on an open patch of ground extending along the line of cliffs, he saw a branch bend back . . . a figure emerge.

The distance was a little more than two hundred yards. In the brief period of time that the figure had been visible, Matt had been unable to determine much about it. A man . . . no doubt about that. But the figure had blended itself with the surroundings. One thing for sure . . . it was a man on foot. The next time Matt caught sight of the figure, it had proceeded a good fifty yards . . . moving fast and silently.

Suddenly the hair stood up on the back of Matt's neck. Whoever it was . . . the figure was moving in the priest's direction. Two missing men . . . and now someone . . . a wraithlike figure moving silently and quickly through the undergrowth . . . was following the priest.

Matt knew he couldn't tarry. Yet, he had no plan of action. What to do? Now the figure stopped at a point of rock and looked out on the country below . . . obviously watching the priest. Suddenly the adrenaline boiled through Matt's veins. Matt had never seen an Apache Indian, but he had seen drawings of them . . . illustrations in newspapers. The lone figure, crouched across the gully, was an Apache warrior. Matt knew it. He knew he was looking at the real thing.

The figure moved . . . disappeared. Matt's mind raced. Should he try to overtake the Indian? Immediately he realized that he would make a great deal of noise if he hurried his horse through the rough country. Perhaps, he told himself, he should merely ride as fast as possible toward the priest . . . warn him . . . join him so they would at least be two against the Apache.

Confusion washed over Matt . . . a measure of fear, too.

He had very little information on Apache . . . information that he could use. He *did* know that they were generally considered among the most fearsome and cunning warriors in all of human history. Masters of guerrilla warfare . . . tireless, vicious, too. He had only one advantage that he could think of. He had seen the Apache . . . the Apache had not seen him.

Matt shook the reins . . . urged the horse forward. He tried to keep the animal out of the rockiest ground, hoping to minimize the sound of his progress. He angled down the slope . . . stopped at the edge of a small, boulder-strewn streambed. Looked up the side of the incline ahead.

Matt wondered where the Apache had gone. He let his eyes go to the higher ground and the point of cliffs. Nothing. He listened. No sound, either.

Matt could feel the pounding of his heart. He slid the rifle out of the saddle holster. Shook the reins and started up toward the place where the base of the cliffs met the steep slope of ground . . . worked his way in and out of the thick stands of juniper.

Once at the base of the cliffs, Matt slid quietly out of the saddle . . . proceeded on foot around a jumble of loose boulders until he reached the crest of the ridge. Now he was in amongst an ancient upheaval of granite . . . strata that had been turned on its side by the slow and grinding movements of early earth. He scanned the country below, hoping to catch sight of the padre. He studied the gully . . . the distant ridge . . . the yawning canyon below. Waited. No priest.

He listened, too . . . hoping to hear the noise of rocks being dislodged by horse's hooves. But the awesome country was immersed in silence.

The force hit Matt with a crushing impact . . . flattening him facedown in the rocky ground. The rifle flew from his grasp. Something hard and sinewy was wrapped around his throat . . . an arm . . . he knew it was an arm, although he couldn't see it. He felt a knee against his back, the full weight of its owner pressing down. Then, out of the corner of his eye, he perceived the dark hand and the foot-long skinning knife poised in the air. Dead. In a sudden rush of thought only that single word flashed down the corridors of Matt Ramsey's mind. I am dead, he told himself.

# CHAPTER

# ★ 14 ★

One mistake. That's what they had been telling him ever since he was big enough to wear britches. Every man makes mistakes, they told him . . . lots of mistakes. Most mistakes can be tolerated, corrected, or just plain forgotten with time. But there is one mistake out of the multitude that must be avoided. That, they told him, is the one big fatal mistake. And Matt Ramsey was dead sure he had just made it.

Below the hard muscle and bone of the arm that was pressed just under Matt's chin was a stretch of taut and totally exposed throat. That, he told himself, was where the blade of the knife would slice. One quick and soundless swipe and it would all be over. Matt knew how the mistake had occurred. He had forgotten about himself. A long time ago someone had told him, "You can't be of any use to anyone else unless you take care of yourself first. The man who fails to take care of his own health, welfare, and safety ain't goin' to be in a position to be of much service to anyone else." For a few moments Matt Ramsey had forgotten about his own welfare, and he was certain he was about to pay the supreme price for the slip. He had wanted to please Alicia by keeping a good eye on the padre . . . wanted to make sure nothing happened to the man. And he had gotten careless. Now, he told himself, he would have to pay.

He wondered why nothing had happened. Of course, it had only been a few seconds . . . no more than that. But why hadn't the blade come down? Then he felt the pressure against his throat easing . . . the weight on his back lifting. The arm let go of his neck entirely, and whoever it was that had been on top of him stood up.

The canyon was as silent as before. Slowly Matt rolled to his side and looked back over his shoulder. What he saw was the most purely aboriginal being he had ever laid eyes on. Long, jet black hair, nearly waist-length and restrained by a band of blue cloth, fell forward of his shoulders. The eyes, framed by a heavy brow and high cheekbones, were narrow . . . their irises nearly as dark as the warrior's hair. The mouth was a grim, narrow-lipped slash beneath a hawk-like nose. The Apache wore only a dirty loincloth, a ragged shirt, and a pair of soft, handmade, knee-high moccasins.

Matt's glance went back to the knife. The almost needle-sharp point was aimed toward his chest . . . or maybe it was his neck. No matter. It *was* aimed at him . . . and the tense, muscled body that held the knife was poised like a taut spring waiting to be unleashed.

Then Matt saw the metal plate pinned to the shirt. It was a small plate of gray metal with a single star cast on its surface. The symbol of the Lone Star State . . . a plate like the plate he and all the men of his regiment had worn on their caps during the war. He saw also the initials *C.M.* scratched deep in the surface near the lower, right-hand corner. C.M., for Cleve Madison. Matt had felt a momentary surge of relief when the Apache released him. Now, like a great, returning wave of doom, the fear washed back over him. Matt looked deep into the dark sockets that held the Indian's eyes, and as he did, Matt Ramsey was convinced that he was looking into the eyes of the man who had killed Cleve Madison.

Matt Ramsey had been surprised by the silent and unsuspected attack, but he was even more surprised by what happened next. The dark lips parted only slightly, and the words came out . . . words that rattled up from deep in the Indian's throat. "I mean you no harm, Ramsey."

Matt was stunned. How could this mountain aboriginal know his name? Fear and confusion intermingled and raced back and forth all through Matt's body. He continued to stare into the deep-set eyes.

In surprisingly good English . . . soft and guttural but almost devoid of an accent . . . the Apache spoke again and relaxed his stance just a little as he did. "Señora Montoya told me that you are Madison's friend."

Matt decided it would be wise to acknowledge the truth of the Indian's statement. He nodded his head . . . rolled over all the way and pushed himself to a sitting position.

Now the Indian stood to his full height and slid the wicked-looking knife into a scabbard. "I meant you no harm. I knew you were following me. You might have shot me." The Indian paused for a moment . . . then a slight smile formed at one corner of his mouth. "Eh?"

Suddenly the fear left Matt. He couldn't figure it all out, but he felt confident that the Apache, as he said, meant him no harm. Matt smiled, too. "I might have done that," he replied.

Matt got to his feet, spit some sand from his mouth, wiped the palms of his hands against his trousers . . . all the while studying the Apache. "You know me, but I don't know you."

The slight smile stayed at the corner of the Indian's mouth. "If I were to tell you my Apache name, you could not say it. White men cannot wrap their tongues around our language. That is why the white men gave me another name. I am known as Cobre. When I asked them why they called me that, they told me it was because my skin was the color of copper. *Cobre* is the Spanish word for 'copper.'"

Matt's knee was throbbing from being knocked to the ground. He limped a few steps, trying it out. Then he pointed to a large flat rock near the base of the cliff. "Think I better set a spell," he told the Apache.

The afternoon sun was bearing down, and the rock was back in the shade. Matt took a seat and massaged the place where his knee had made harsh contact with the rocky soil. Cobre squatted on the ground in front of him.

While Matt rubbed at the side of his kneecap, he studied Cobre. The Indian picked idly at a scab on the point of his shin . . . looked up at Matt from time to time. Finally Matt spoke. "How do you know Señora Montoya? You said she told you that I was Cleve Madison's friend."

"She brings food and other supplies for me and leaves them at the base of the cliffs that are shaped like the tail of an eagle. Have you seen these cliffs?"

"No," said Matt.

"They are at the edge of the valley no more than two miles from Madison's place. Sometimes I wait there for her and we talk. I had seen you riding with Madison's squaw. So I asked Señora Montoya who you were."

Matt nodded thoughtfully. The Indian's answer told him something, but it didn't tell him everything. He wondered if he could converse with Cobre as he would with a white man. Could he talk to him in a straightforward manner? Might as well try, Matt told himself. "Tell me, Cobre," he said, "tell me how you came to know Cleve Madison."

Cobre was silent for a time, picking at the scab. "He is my friend," he finally said.

The answer was direct, but it didn't tell him all he desired to know. "How did you become friends?"

Again, Cobre was a long time in answering. He stood up. "That is a story that is long in telling. Come, you can go to my camp. I have fresh meat. Tonight, as we sit at my campfire, I will tell the story."

Matt got up from the rock. "I'm supposed to keep an eye on the padre. Make sure nothin' happens to him. I probably should stay on his trail."

"I know where he is going," said Cobre. "No reason for you to follow. If you want to see him, we can see him tomorrow. I will take you to the place where he will be."

"You know where he is going?"

"Yes," said Cobre. "He makes his way by looking at a map. But I do not need a map. He is trying to reach the place where the big bell lies among the boulders of an arroyo. The trail to that place is old and has not been used for a very long time. The black robe's eyes cannot see the old trail. My eyes can see it."

"Do you know where the bell is?" asked Matt.

"Yes, I know," Cobre told him. "But the black robe must not go to the place of the bell."

"Why?" Matt inquired.

"That is where the crazy gold is buried. He cannot go there."

"Why do you call it crazy gold?" asked Matt.

"Because it makes white men go crazy. It makes them kill each other and mistreat the Indians. It draws other white men like flies are drawn to dung. They come and take the land, ruin everything. These mountains are sacred Apache ground. Long ago my people drove the black robes away and made the land as it had been before their coming. That is why the black robe must not find the great bell."

Matt was beginning to understand. "You say he must not find the bell. Will you prevent him from finding it?"

"Yes," said Cobre.

"How will you do that?"

Cobre did not hesitate. He looked directly into Matt's eyes. "I will kill him."

"Would you kill me?" asked Matt.

"You are Madison's friend. Madison would never try to find the bell or dig for the crazy gold. He told me so, long ago. If you are his friend, as you say you are, then you would not try to find it, either. As long as you remain Madison's friend, I will not kill you."

Matt almost smiled. Cobre was, in his aboriginal fashion, a diplomat. What Matt took from Cobre's remarks was this: If he stayed away from the bell and stayed away from the gold, he would stay alive. "Tell me," said Matt, "how long will it take the priest to get to the place where the bell is located?"

"All of this day . . . all of the next day. If he could see the trail as I can, he could get there early in the morning."

Matt stood in deep thought. His job was to protect the priest. Perhaps, he told himself, it *would* be a good idea to go to Cobre's camp. Maybe there was some way he and

Cobre could come up with a plan that would save the priest and satisfy the Indian. "I was sent into these mountains by Madison's wife. My job is to protect the priest . . . to see that no harm comes to him."

Cobre thought about it for a moment. Then he shrugged his shoulders, nothing more.

Matt thought he might try to approach the matter from another angle. "Mrs. Madison has been told by the priest that he is trying to find the mission so . . ." Matt's voice trailed off. He was wondering if the Indian could understand or appreciate what he would tell him. "The priest told Mrs. Madison, as he told me, that he's trying to locate the old mission so his church can someday build a monument where it once stood." Matt stopped . . . looked into Cobre's eyes.

Cobre did not speak nor in any way change his expression. After a long moment of silence the Indian reached up and pressed a finger to his chest as though indicating his heart. "In here," said Cobre, "I know that the black robe speaks falsely to you and the squaw. He seeks the gold."

Matt's brow wrinkled. Now, what could he say to the Indian? How do you argue with intuitive thoughts? "If the priest finds the bell, then leaves and gives me and Mrs. Madison his word that he will not return or bring others into the mountains . . . would you permit him to leave with his life?"

Cobre pointed to Matt's rifle, lying some yards away in the dirt. "We can ride to my camp. I will listen to you, Ramsey. I will think on all you say. And we can speak about our friend, Madison. Wait here." Then, without another word, the Apache turned, climbed to the top of the forty-foot cliffs, and disappeared.

Matt walked slowly back to the spot where he had tied his horse. He took a long drink of water, then sat on the shady side of a low-growing juniper. In less than five minutes, he heard the soft crunch of hooves, and Cobre, mounted, rode out of a nearby gully. The saddle on the horse was of Mexican styling, and the brand on the animal was not Madison's Circle M. Now Cobre wore a cartridge belt with two holstered pistols. A bandolier of ammunition was slung across his chest and he carried a repeating rifle in his free hand.

As Matt swung into the saddle, he asked Cobre a question. "Do you know anything of Cleve Madison's disappearance?"

Cobre shook his head from side to side. "I have looked through all the canyons of the Baboquivaris. All the way north . . . beyond Coyotero arroyo . . . down the west side of the mountains to Pan Tak and the villages of the Pimas . . . all the way south to the place where the Mexicans are camped."

"Mexicans? Where are Mexicans camped?"

"That way," said Cobre, pointing in a southerly direction.

"How many?"

Cobre wrinkled his brow for a moment. Then he held up all of his fingers. "This many." Then he closed his hands and held up four fingers. "And this many."

"Fourteen," said Matt. Now his brow wrinkled. "How long have they been camped there?"

"I do not know," replied Cobre. "Maybe they have been there a long time. I saw them first"—he held up nine fingers—"that many days ago."

"Tell me as best you can exactly where they are camped."

"To the south . . . near the place where the Baboquivaris come down to the valley and disappear into the ground."

"Where the mountains end?" asked Matt.

"Yes . . . where the mountains end. The Mexicans are up in the mountains . . . in a large valley between two low peaks. The Mexicans and their mules."

"Mules? The Mexicans have mules?"

Cobre held his fists up again . . . opened and closed them twice. "That many mules."

Matt thought about it for a minute. "Why so many mules?"

Again, Cobre touched a finger to his chest. "To carry the crazy gold down from the mountains."

Matt had a feeling, too . . . and his feeling was in agreement with Cobre's. "Have you ever seen Mexicans in these mountains before . . . lots of Mexicans with mules?" Cobre shook his head from side to side. "Maybe these Mexicans are woodcutters." Once more Cobre shook his head in the negative. "Have you watched them?" Matt asked.

"I watched them for all of one day," said Cobre. "They do no work . . . only sit in the shade and smoke. Some sleep."

Matt was thinking of the mysterious, unnamed, and supposedly wealthy Mexican rancher. According to information from McNeal and Alicia, the Mexican rancher first tried to lease Baboquivari land from Madison, then later tried to make an agreement with McNeal. Ambitious men . . . men with greed . . . don't give up easy, Matt told himself. Matt had a strange feeling that the Indian might be right. "Will you take me to the place where the Mexicans are camped?"

"Yes," said Cobre. He pointed toward the south. "My camp is that way. We can leave my camp at the first morning light . . . ride the high ridges and reach the Mexican camp before darkness. Then, with the light of the next day, you can watch them. That's what you want to do, eh, Ramsey?"

"Yes."

"We can watch one day . . . no more. Then I must return to kill the black robe." Cobre touched the flanks of his horse gently . . . turned it with the reins. Matt followed. They angled away from the ragged cliffs, heading for a deep canyon that flowed toward the south.

# CHAPTER

## ★ 15 ★

Darkness came to the deep canyons of the Baboquivaris as though a curtain had been drawn. This quick and enveloping phenomenon occurred only moments after the sun's rays were cut off by the highest peaks.

Cobre had built a small fire, good for cooking and helpful in moving around. However, only a few feet from the glowing coals the light from the fire was overpowered by the night.

They were in a deep and precipitous canyon . . . a gorge they had accessed by riding down a twisting trail that, at times, fell off on the canyon side for a hundred feet or more. Cobre's camp was a crude and primitive affair. There was a semblance of a shelter, but it was nothing more than a lean-to built out from a place where a shelf of rock protruded from the canyon wall. Then there was the crude fireplace and a mound of charcoal and ashes . . . a freshly killed deer carcass hanging from a tripod of poles. That was about it.

Cobre, in the darkness, cooked strips of fresh venison . . . laid out piñon nuts and a type of dried bean that Matt did not recognize nor intend to eat. Matt, in turn, contributed one of Alicia's food parcels. Cobre had some coffee, and he brewed it in a pan over the open fire. "Señora Montoya brought this coffee," Cobre told Matt.

They prepared the meal in relative silence . . . sat and ate in much the same way. Matt wanted to hear Cobre's story . . . the story about how he had become friends with Cleve Madison. But he assumed that Cobre would tell the story when he was ready to do so.

After Cobre had finished eating, he tossed some sticks on the coals and sat back on his haunches. Sitting at the bottom of the deep canyon, Matt told himself, was like sitting at the bottom of a well. Matt wondered how Cobre could live in such a lonely and desolate place. He also wondered *why* he lived there. "Are there any other Apache people living in these mountains?" Matt asked.

"No," said Cobre. "All Apache have been taken to the reservation." And that was all he said. He squatted and stared into the fire. After the passage of a good many minutes, Cobre shifted his weight slightly and spoke. "Now I will tell you the story of how I became Madison's friend."

Matt scooted and shifted his weight, trying to get comfortable on the hard and uneven ground around the small campfire. It soon became apparent to Matt that Cobre, in order to explain his friendship to Madison, was actually telling the story of his entire life.

"I was born in a wickiup near the place where two rivers come together. Like all places and all things, the names of these rivers, as I will tell it to you, are Spanish names or names in your language. This is because, as I told you, the white man cannot speak our Apache words, so everything these days is changing."

Cobre picked up some of the piñon nuts and began cracking them with his teeth and eating the tiny bits of white meat contained within the soft shells. "So . . . I was born where the Gila and San Carlos rivers join. Those rivers are in the direction of the morning sun . . . to the east, as you say. Farther up there were great forests, many cold streams, and big mountains that were often covered with deep snow. This was Apache land.

"There were some mines near the place between the rivers. These were mines where the white man dug for crazy gold. When I was a young boy, the white soldiers said that

Apache could no longer go into Mexico to take horses from the *ranchos* of the Mexicans. They said we could not wander as we once had . . . freely over all the land. Many Apache were killed by white soldiers. They said we must stay only on certain land . . . on the reservation. The big camp on the reservation was a place called the agency. The white men and white soldiers stayed at the agency, and Apache went to this place to get food. This was because they took our guns, and we could no longer hunt. They told us to farm, but Apache know nothing of such work."

An owl hooted from some distant spot. Cobre stopped and listened. "I hope that owl does not come too close. Owls are the messengers that bring bad news. If the owl flies over our camp and drops a feather, that means bad news."

They sat quietly. Matt listened with Cobre. But the owl did not hoot again. Matt unfolded some cloth and extended it toward the Indian. "Cookies," said Matt.

Cobre took several and picked up the story where he had left off. "So . . . my father could speak a little of the white man's language. He went to one of the mines and offered to work. For his work we received food and other things. When I grew big enough, I went to the mine with my father to help. I cut wood. I carried water. I fed horses. I learned how to speak the white man's language. When I got even bigger, I rode a wagon to another mine and worked there, too.

"Then, I got a job on a white man's ranch. I herded cattle and put brands on them. My parents finally moved to another place on the reservation, but I stayed at the ranch.

"When I became as tall as I am now, this rancher . . . a man named Olsen . . . told me that the white men at the reservation had a job for Apache who could be trusted and were brave. This job was called scouting. So I went to the agency, and they made me a scout. Since I could speak the white man's language, I was made a sergeant . . . a chief over other scouts.

"Our job was to catch bronco Apache . . . catch Apache that the white man said were bad and causing trouble. I did not like the idea of catching my own people. Sometimes we had to shoot the broncos. Some of the broncos were bad men. Some of them got drunk on tiswin and killed other Apache. But some of the broncos only wanted to raid and take horses. Some wanted to live in the mountains of Mexico, and these would run away."

Matt cut in. "So you were like policemen . . . is that right?"

"Yes," replied Cobre. "After a while, I became proud of my job. I told myself that the way of the future would be the white man's way. I knew that the Apache could never drive the white men from the land. There are too many white men. So I tried to keep peace between the whites and the Apache. I told people not to break the white man's law, and when they did, I took them in. I tried to be fair to all Apache the same. I tried to be a friend to white men, too. I tried to show a good path for all to follow. I wore a blue jacket the same as white soldiers . . . a jacket with yellow stripes on the sleeves."

"Did you live with the white soldiers . . . ride with white soldiers?" Matt inquired.

"Yes. White soldiers cannot find Apache when they run away. But Apache scouts, all wearing blue jackets, can find Apache. So we went ahead of the white soldiers and found the broncos wherever they were hiding. We got good food and white man's money for doing this work."

Matt wondered why Cobre was no longer working as a scout. But he was sure that he would find that out as Cobre's story revealed further events of his life. It was, in Matt's opinion, the long way around to find out how Cobre had become Cleve Madison's friend, but Matt also figured that there was little else to do in the dark confines of the Baboquivaris. Besides, the story of Cobre's life interested him.

"One day," said Cobre as he continued, "I was told to lead a group of white soldiers to find some very bad broncos. These broncos had killed some Apache squaws and children. Since I am now chief of all Apache scouts, the captain told me to go with the soldiers because the broncos were hiding in some big canyons, and the captain knew that I could find them.

"The leader of these soldiers was named Hayes. He had two gold bars on his jacket, and he drank too much whiskey. He drank whiskey while we were riding to this place called Cibicue where there was an Apache camp. This was the place where the broncos had gone. Hayes gave some of the soldiers whiskey, too. Pretty soon those soldiers were drunk."

Cobre stopped to crack a piñon nut, and Matt poured himself some coffee out of the battered pan. "How many soldiers were there?" Matt inquired.

"Two squads," replied Cobre. "When we got to the camp, the soldiers stayed away and I went in alone. No broncos. Only some women and children. The broncos were gone. I walked out in the clearing and called to the soldiers. They came and brought my horse. I got on, and we started to leave. Then a dog ran out and started barking. The dog was barking at Hayes's horse, and the horse made noise and jumped around. Then Hayes took out his pistol and shot the dog. The sound of the gun frightened a woman, and she screamed. Hayes was very mad. He shot at the woman, and she ran. Then other soldiers started shooting at the woman. Other women and children started running. The drunk soldiers ran their horses through the camp."

"Holy shit," Matt interjected.

"A woman fell down with blood all over her face. I started yelling at the soldiers. Another woman fell dead. Then they killed a young boy. Then everybody started shooting. I yelled at Hayes. I told him to stop. He looked at me with hate and pointed his pistol at me. I kicked my horse and rode into the trees. I was ashamed of the blue jacket. I tore it off. I could hear the women and children screaming. Every soldier was shooting now."

Matt felt nearly sick to his stomach. He had heard similar tales before. "I'm sorry to hear this," he told Cobre.

"I took my rifle and started shooting at the soldiers. I killed three of them. Then they all turned their guns on me.

The forest was very thick with trees, so I rode into the trees and lost them.

"After the soldiers had gone, I went back to the camp. Many of the women and children were dead. Many were wounded so bad they would die. I was very angry with those soldiers, so I rode after them. These were not good soldiers, and they were drunk, so it was easy for me to ride the high ground and shoot down on them. I killed more of them. Then, as the sun went behind the mountains, they became very frightened and started running their horses. I followed and one by one I killed them. I killed Hayes, and then there were only two left. I killed one of those soldiers, but one soldier rode into the agency where I could not get him."

Cobre stopped and sat silently for a few moments. Then he poured some coffee for himself.

"I bet I know what happened next," said Matt. "The man who made it back to the agency told lies to protect his own skin."

"That's right, Ramsey. The captain told all the soldiers to kill me. Every soldier rode out. They called for other soldiers from other places. Soldiers rode out from Fort Thomas, from Fort Apache, from Fort McDowell. Pretty soon all the hills were covered with soldiers. Then the law started looking for me. Many men rode out to join the soldiers. But I rode quickly to the Chiricahua Mountains. No white man can find an Apache in the Chiricahuas. But soon they knew I was hiding there, and soldiers were everyplace. Then they put put my face on pieces of paper and put them in every town. They said they would give a lot of white man's money to anyone who killed me."

"There was a reward for you, is that what you're saying?" Matt asked.

"That is true," said Cobre. "So I slipped out of the Chiricahuas and rode west to Madison's place. He was my friend, and I knew he would help me."

Matt cut in. "You already knew Cleve Madison when this happened? How did you know him?"

"A long time ago, before this trouble happened, I was with some soldiers down this way. We were tracking some broncos who had gone into Mexico to steal horses. I was far ahead of the soldiers because they must always stop to rest. I was on this little mountain, and I heard rifle shots. I rode over the mountain, and I saw one white man hiding in some rocks." Cobre held up six fingers. "This many broncos were there, and they were shooting at the white man. I got off my horse and climbed into the rocks behind the broncos. I killed four of them, and the others rode off."

"The white man was Cleve Madison," said Matt.

"That is true," said Cobre. "And that is how we became friends."

"I can almost figure the rest of it," said Matt. "You needed a place to hide, and Cleve helped you. Don't the soldiers ever come in here looking for you?"

"No," said Cobre. "No one knows that I am in these mountains. Only Madison, his squaw, and Señora Montoya know that I am here. Soldiers could not catch me in these mountains, even if all the soldiers from all the forts came searching."

"I can believe that," said Matt. "I've been all over the Rockies, but these mountains—foot for foot—are rougher than the Rockies." The two of them sat quietly for a moment. "Anyway," Matt went on, "you've told me how you became friends with Cleve. He's my friend, also. What do you think, Cobre . . . do you think he's dead?"

Cobre sat for a long time. Finally he shook his head from side to side. He did not know.

"Well," said Matt, "I don't know, either. I'm very anxious to see those Mexicans with the mules."

Cobre rose from his place by the fire. He pointed toward the lean-to. "My blanket is there," he said.

"I'll roll out my bedroll right here," said Matt.

A few minutes later Matt was lying in his bedroll, looking up through the darkest night he had ever experienced . . . looking into a field of countless glittering specks. Never, he told himself, had he ever seen such a concentration of stars. Somewhere up the canyon the owl hooted. Matt Ramsey was not a superstitious man, but he wished the owl would go away.

# CHAPTER
## ★16★

Cobre's movements roused Matt in the inky darkness of the canyon night. He rolled over and looked out from his bedroll. The Indian was digging in the fireplace with a stick. Then he tossed a few pieces of kindling and some dead grass onto the previous evening's fire. Afterward, he knelt by the fireplace and began blowing gently. An eerie glow from the awakened coals spread across the Apache's rugged countenance, and shortly, the dead grass flamed.

Matt rolled out of the blankets. Damn, he told himself, Alicia was right. The canyon's early-morning cold seeped through his clothes. He pulled on his boots, then went to the place where he had placed the saddle and his other belongings. The warmth of the jacket felt good.

Cobre was squatting by the fire, his opened palms extended over the bright flames. Matt took another food parcel from a saddlebag, returned to the fire, and crouched across from Cobre. "We gonna leave in darkness?" Matt asked.

Cobre nodded. Matt opened the parcel. Inside were strips of dried beef and cold biscuits. He extended it to Cobre and afterward helped himself. Matt was thinking about the steep drop-offs along the twisting trail that had brought them into the canyon. "We goin' out the same way we came in?"

"No," said Cobre, chewing at a piece of jerky.

That made Matt feel a little better. On the other hand, he told himself, the way out might be worse than the way in. Nothing to do but wait and see.

The tiny fire burned down. They finished eating, then saddled up the mounts. "This ride will take all day. Is that what you said?" Matt inquired.

"All day," replied Cobre, swinging into the saddle. Cobre wasn't much inclined to elaborate, Matt told himself. Sharp contrast compared to Cobre's storytelling of the night past. Oh, well, Matt thought, maybe Indians are like white men in at least one regard. Maybe it takes them a little while to wake up in the morning.

The path out was *not* as bad as the path in. For a good distance they followed the canyon in an upstream direction, ascending higher and higher into the Baboquivaris. As they rode in near total darkness, Matt, unable to see the ground beneath the horse's hooves, put his trust entirely in Cobre and his buckskin. Cobre moved through the jagged twists and turns of the canyon without the slightest hesitation. Moving like a man moves down the hall of a house he has lived in for twenty years, Matt thought to himself. Matt supposed that Cobre knew the Baboquivaris just about that well.

At a suitable spot Cobre turned his mount out of the streambed and angled up the side of the canyon. By the light of earliest day, Matt could see the irregular line far above where the pine trees began. Right now they were moving through loose shale and scattered juniper trees. Matt had no idea where they were relative to the priest's position. He would leave that to Cobre.

Matt, riding behind, studied the Apache. Most likely, he told himself, the Indian had never cut his hair . . . probably not ever . . . probably not even as a child. Matt smiled to himself. How would he know that? Just a time-passing guess . . . just something to kill the boredom of a long and tedious ride. Matt had heard that Apache warriors could run fifty miles in a single day . . . exist by eating only the nuts and seeds they might accumulate along the way. They could do this all day without water, he had been told. Matt was damn glad the Indian had become his friend. He wouldn't want him for an enemy.

After a while Matt removed the jacket. By now the rays of morning sun had spilled all across the eastern side of the Baboquivaris. Its warmth felt good across Matt's back. He wondered if the Indian owned a jacket . . . or ever wore one.

By midmorning they were into the pine country, and before noon the horses had topped out on one of the north-south ridges. Now the riding was easier. They were moving on level ground, which was covered, in many places, by low-growing grass and pine needles.

When they reached Baboquivari Peak, which jutted up another fifteen hundred feet, Cobre stayed at their present elevation and guided his horse on a level path around the peak. Matt was almost dozing under the warm sun when the thought impacted his mind. "Oh, shit," he muttered under his breath. Then, in a much louder voice, "Cobre."

The Apache, riding twenty paces ahead, reined his horse, turned, and waited for Matt to catch up. "You need rest?" Cobre asked.

"No," said Matt.

"Soldiers always need rest. Hard to catch broncos when soldiers along. They always say, we need rest. Then broncos get away."

Matt smiled. "There's something I need to ask you. Somehow it didn't occur to me before. Was the priest alone when you first spotted him?"

Cobre nodded in the affirmative. "Soldiers sleep too much, too. Cobre always shaking soldiers. Get up. Get up, I say. Broncos are riding in darkness. Soldiers sleep."

"Do you know Bob Whipple? He's a young cowboy on Madison's ranch."

"I have seen him from a distance," Cobre replied.

"Bob came into the mountains with the priest the first time. But he didn't come out. The priest said they got separated. You never saw anyone but the priest?"

"Only the black robe," Cobre told him.

Matt sat quietly . . . thinking. He turned back to Cobre. "How did you spot the priest in the first place?"

"Boom . . . boom!" said Cobre. "Cobre is way up here . . . back there." He pointed toward the north. "I hear the gun two times, but in these mountains the sound runs all around . . . comes back many times. But I ride down the mountain . . . wait for night . . . see campfire. See the black robe."

"You heard two shots?" Cobre nodded. Matt lapsed into thought. Two gun shots. One for a man . . . one for the man's horse. Of course, Matt told himself, there were plenty of other reasons for a weapon to be discharged. Maybe Bob and the priest had run across some game. Maybe Bob was just breaking the monotony by shooting at a dead tree limb. The priest carried a rifle in his saddle holster. Maybe after Bob and the priest became separated, the priest had fired his rifle in an attempt to let Bob know where he was. Still . . . "Tell me something," Matt said. "If one man killed another in these mountains, could you find the body?"

Cobre's brow wrinkled. He thought about it . . . finally shrugged his shoulders. After another long period of silence, he spoke. "If body is lying right there"—he pointed to the ground a few feet away—"and I come riding by, I would find body. But . . . Ramsey . . ." This time the Indian turned in a slow circle and swept his arm from north to south. "Many things are dead in these mountains right now, and I will never see them. Dead deer . . . dead lion . . . dead squirrel. I will never see those things."

Matt understood what Cobre was saying. The mountains were too vast . . . too many canyons . . . deep gullies . . . caves and brushy draws. Matt thought about it some more. It seemed to him that there was a thread of some sort that was trying to tie a number of events together. Mexicans with mules to the south . . . a priest who, according to Cobre's intuitive opinion, was trying to locate a hoard of gold . . . and two missing men.

"You want to rest?" Cobre asked.

Matt smiled at him. The Apache apparently had a low level of respect for the white man's endurance. "No," Matt replied, reaching for his water flask. "Let's take a drink and head on." Matt finished drinking and held the leather flask toward Cobre. The Indian shook his head. He didn't need any water. "Well, let's be going," Matt said. "I'm anxious to get a look at the Mexicans."

They rode on, not stopping even at midday. But from time to time Cobre would dismount and walk. He advised Matt to do the same. "Horse like soldiers. Need rest."

As he walked, Matt removed some food from the saddlebag. He ate as he walked. Once during the day he saw Cobre remove a leather pouch from his saddle horn. The Indian reached into the pouch . . . removed a handful of something and tossed it into his mouth. Seeds, Matt figured.

By midafternoon Matt was tired to the bone. Don't be stupid, he told himself, you're no Apache. "Hey, Cobre," he called. The Indian stopped. "I need to tell you something. Many years ago I was a soldier."

The tiny smile, seen only once before by Matt, returned to the corner of Cobre's mouth. He pointed to a shady spot under a big pine. "Sit down, Ramsey. You need rest."

After sitting for perhaps fifteen minutes, Matt asked Cobre, "How much farther?"

The Indian looked up at the sun. From their place on the ridge it was possible to look out to the west across a vast sprawl of desert that stretched to a distant horizon. Cobre pointed to the horizon. "When the sun sits on those far mountains, we will be there."

Matt looked from the sun's position to the horizon. About five or six more hours, he figured. "Well, let's move on," he said.

Eventually they reached a place where a point of cliffs looked down on a long ridge that sloped toward the south. From their present position, Matt could look to the horizon in three directions. Off to the east the Altar Valley and Madison's grazing land undulated gently toward Tubac and the Santa Cruz River. To the west the land was flat and parched. To the south the mountains continued, but they were dropping off, each ensuing peak lower than its northern neighbor. Finally, about fifteen miles in that direction, the foothills of the Baboquivaris blended into the lowland desert.

Cobre pointed south and a little to the east. "You see that place down there where many tall rocks stand up?"

Matt squinted his eyes in the harsh light. "I think so. You mean that line of rocks way over there?"

"Yes," said Cobre. "Those are ancient giants turned to stone." Matt nodded thoughtfully. The rocks did, indeed, look like a long line of human figures. Well, almost like human figures, Matt told himself. "We will ride to that place and leave the horses. Don't take horses too close. Mexican horses and mules smell our horses, they can make big racket. Not good."

Matt understood. "Where are the Mexicans?"

Cobre pointed more directly toward the south. "Between those two peaks is a valley. Grass for animals. That place is where the Mexicans make camp."

They continued on. In the softening light of late afternoon Alicia's tanned features and blue-gray eyes moved through the corridors of Matt Ramsey's mind. Then he recalled something. He had had a dream the night previous . . . sleeping on the hard rocks of Cobre's hidden canyon camp. Like most dreams, the contents of this one escaped Matt's recall. But it had been a dream about Alicia. For a good distance Matt tried to bring the dream back, but it stubbornly resisted. For some reason the residue of the dream and the mental recall of Alicia's face caused Matt to feel something strong and compelling. What was it exactly? he asked himself. What was it he was feeling? The word *longing* came to his mind. Yes, he told himself . . . he was longing for Alicia. "Damn."

He said it loud enough that Cobre's keen ears picked it up. The Indian turned in the saddle and glanced back, then turned his attention back to the trail. Matt smiled. He wondered if Cobre, confined to the wild and lonesome reaches of the Baboquivaris dreamed of dark-eyed Indian maidens in some far distant encampment. Probably, he told himself.

They started angling down a steep incline to a hogback ridge some five hundred feet below. The horses picked up the pace, snorted and showed excitement. Just before they hit the hogback, Cobre reined his mount hard to the left, and there, spilling out of a narrow crevasse in a wall of rock, was a cascade of fresh mountain water.

Matt dismounted and watched as the horses drank from the pool at the base of the rock. Cobre went to his knees and drank, also. When he stood up, Matt asked him, "Did you know that the water was here?"

Cobre gave him a strange look. "How can a man live in the land if he does not know where the water is?"

Although Cobre answered his question with a question, Matt understood. Matt took both his water flasks from the saddle and filled them at the small waterfall.

After all thirsts had been slaked, they mounted and rode on. They arrived at the place where the "people turned to stone" were standing at almost the very instant that the sun touched the western horizon. Matt shook his head in amazement. Cobre has estimated their arrival almost precisely. Cobre, Matt decided, was a valuable find.

They camped at the feet of one of the "petrified giants." Cobre prepared a small rock fireplace. Matt gathered dried wood. Then they sat in darkness and ate more biscuits and dried beef. Cobre shared some piñon nuts with Matt. Cobre seemed disinclined to talk very much. In fact, except for the detailed story of his life and adventures as told the night before, Cobre, in Matt's estimation, was a man of few words.

When the fire had burned down to coals, Matt looked up at the towering stone monolith. "You said those are people turned to stone. How did that happen?"

Cobre, looking into the fire, did not even raise his eyes. "They were out of harmony." He said no more. As usual, Matt mused, Cobre's answer came quickly and was straight-forward in its context. But it didn't tell Matt all he wanted to know. Maybe white men want to know too much, Matt conjectured. Maybe we waste a lot of time goin' into a lot of details we don't really need. Matt thought that would be all from Cobre. But after a few moments of silence the Apache spoke again. "That's what some people think. I think they are black robes and Spaniards who mistreated the Indians."

Matt looked across at Cobre. He was sure the Apache bore a deep, lifelong resentment against those who had moved into the land without being invited. "Tell me Cobre," Matt inquired, "do you dislike all white men?"

Cobre shook his head from side to side. "No. I like some white men. I would just feel better if you all went away."

Matt smiled in the darkness. Cobre was not a man to beat around the bush. "But Cleve Madison is your friend, eh?"

"Yes," Cobre replied.

"I am your friend, also," Matt said.

"Good," said Cobre. Then he pointed a long, bony finger across the fire and in a general northerly direction. "But do not ever go into the Baboquivaris looking for the buried gold."

"No," said Matt, "I wouldn't do that." A shiver ran up his spine. Cobre would kill him in an instant if he ever found him digging in the vicinity of the big bell, wherever it might be.

They sat without speaking for another few minutes. Then without a formal good-night—or even a good-night of any kind—Cobre drew his ragged blanket around him and stretched out on the ground. Matt did likewise. He was dead tired from nearly eighteen hours of travel, and he had a few lingering aches from Cobre's assault of the previous afternoon. Before he lapsed into a deep sleep, Matt wondered when that long-anticipated but never realized stretch of lazy days would come his way. That's what he had expected when he came to the Circle M, but it hadn't worked out that way. His mind, slowly . . . gently, shutting down for sleep, recalled the day he and Alicia had stopped in the clearing and had their picnic with the quail calling in the brush and the bees humming in the mesquite trees. That had been slow and easy. He saw her face again as he had seen it earlier in the day. But this time tears were welling up in her eyes. She leaned toward him, and he put his arm around her shoulder. She raised her face and looked tenderly into his eyes. The dream began. In the morning he would remember none of it.

# CHAPTER
## ★ 17 ★

For reasons unknown to Matt, Cobre did not awake in darkness as he had the previous morning. The Indian slept until the sun was fully up. So did Matt. He had needed a good night's rest, and the ground in pine country was considerably more comfortable than the rocky ground of Cobre's canyon.

They rode the ridges directly south for what seemed to Matt to be about six or seven miles. Then Cobre stopped. "We leave the horses here," he said.

Both removed the saddles from their horses. Each carried his rifle when they left. They made good time going downhill. But Matt reminded himself that at the end of the day the return trip would be uphill.

Late in the morning Cobre stopped in a thicket of small, scrubby junipers. They were out of the pine country now, and the terrain was again convoluted and tossed. Cobre pointed to the south. "Mexicans are that way. You stay close to me. Walk quiet."

Matt did as the Indian suggested. Cobre angled toward a shallow ravine and entered it, then went up and over a hump of boulder-strewn ground that gave way to another heavily eroded ravine. He stopped again . . . waited for Matt to catch up. This time he whispered, "Voices go long way here." Matt nodded his understanding. "Walk low to ground. We go to those rocks." He pointed to a group of huge granite boulders—some nearly as big as small houses—all piled one atop another.

They worked their way up through the boulders to a point where they had good concealment but an unobstructed view of the valley below. Cobre poked his head above the rocky rampart. In a moment he hunched down and whispered to Matt, "You look."

Cautiously Matt eased his head above the boulder. Before him and about four hundred yards away was the Mexican camp. It was much as Cobre had described it. A sizable, grassy valley surrounded by hills on three sides. There was heavy juniper growth at the edge of the valley, but only grass farther out. Horses and mules were grazing. Across the valley and close to the line of trees was the Mexican encampment. In several places ground cloths had been strung between small juniper trees to serve as shelters. Matt could see bedrolls laid out . . . saddles on the ground . . . a large rock fireplace for cooking.

First, Matt counted the mules. There were twenty, just as Cobre had indicated. Then horses. Fourteen horses. Finally he counted men. Eleven. Cobre had said fourteen. But as he watched, two men came out of the trees carrying wood. After a while another figure, apparently taking a siesta under one of the shelters, showed himself. Fourteen.

Matt eased back down. He sat in silence for a long time. Cobre watched him but said nothing. Finally Matt spoke. "I think you're right, Cobre. These men are waitin' for something. I can think of only one thing that they could be waitin' for. They must be waitin' for the priest to locate the mission. All those mules tell me that they are plannin' on a heavy load goin' back to Mexico."

Cobre nodded his agreement.

Matt thought about it some more. "But I must tell you, Cobre, I am not totally sure about what I just said. We need to do somethin' . . . take some action . . . but I'm not sure, just yet, what that might be."

"Kill the black robe," said Cobre.

Matt smiled broadly. He almost laughed, but he knew

that he must stifle any noisy outburst. Cobre's suggestion contained a lot of logic. Assume the possibility that the priest was truly seeking the lost gold of San Acacia del Norte. Then kill him. The possibility is erased. A sound method . . . if one was not particular about whether he killed the innocent or the guilty. "I can't do that just yet," said Matt.

"Mexicans are not good fighters," said Cobre. "We can shoot many of them, and the rest will run away."

Matt knew that he had to reason with the Apache, but he wasn't sure of how he should approach the matter. "Cobre, try to understand that the thing that is most important to me is to find my friend Cleve . . . or to find out what happened to Cleve. Do you see what I mean?"

Cobre nodded that he did.

"Also, Cleve—if he ever returns—must live in the Altar Valley for many years among people who try to live by the law. His wife must live there, too . . . and all of the people who work on the ranch. So . . . for their sakes, we must be very careful and not kill innocent people."

Cobre was scowling. Matt waited. Slowly the scowl was replaced by a broad grin. "You speak too many words. I know what you mean before you say so many words. You are saying, make sure before you shoot. That's what you mean."

Now Matt *did* laugh, but he kept it behind closed lips and deep in his throat. He was amused and embarrassed at the same time. Cobre was, without doubt, his mental equal . . . maybe more than that.

All through the day the two of them stayed in the rocks, taking turns at watching the Mexicans. Matt began wondering just what he was trying to accomplish with the watching. He had seen the camp, counted men and horses. He looked at the sun. They had a long walk back to the high country where the horses had been left. It would be nearly dark before they could complete the journey. Yet, something was keeping him at the lookout post in the rocks.

Sometime later Cobre was serving as lookout. Matt was

sprawled on one of the large boulders, resting, his hat across his eyes. Something touched his leg. He raised the brim of the hat. Cobre motioned to him.

Matt crawled up to the lookout point. Now all of the Mexicans were assembled near the fireplace . . . some standing . . . some squatting. It was a meeting of some kind. Both Matt and Cobre watched. The meeting lasted less than five minutes.

After the brief meeting, the Mexicans returned to whatever it was they had been doing before. But one of the group walked out into the valley and collected a horse . . . led it back and saddled it. "One of them is goin' somewhere," Matt said. Cobre nodded.

While the Mexican was preparing the horse, a second Mexican joined him . . . appeared to be talking to him. Then, the first Mexican mounted the horse and rode toward the east. The topography surrounding Matt and Cobre's vantage point cut off their view of the rider shortly after he left the camp. If the Mexican turned south after riding out of the mountains, that would take him to Mexico . . . north would lead to the Altar Valley and Madison land. East? Matt doubted that the Mexican would continue in an easterly direction.

Matt turned to Cobre. "When did you figure that the priest would get to the old mission site?"

"Now," said Cobre.

"Today?"

"Yes, if the map was a good map."

"Could we reach the place where the bell is located today?"

"I could reach it in darkness . . . but you cannot, Ramsey." Cobre pointed toward the high country where the horses had been left. "I could run to horses. Then ride beyond Baboquivari Peak. Then leave horse and go over bad ground with many cliffs. I could go there, but horse cannot."

Matt understood. "Let's start back. I need to think about our next move. When we get to the horses, we can talk about it. What would you do, Cobre?"

Cobre's thoughts hadn't changed since last he expressed them. "Shoot Mexicans . . . go back and kill black robe."

"For all I know, that might be the best thing to do. But I'm not sure it's the right thing. Will you let me think on it while we walk?" Cobre nodded again.

It was nearly dark by the time they reached the horses. Matt hated to admit it, but the long, tough uphill climb had left him nearly exhausted. "Cobre," he said, "maybe I was a soldier too long. I need rest. Let's camp here." And so they did.

Sitting at the small evening campfire, Matt probed Cobre for his thoughts. "Do you have any feeling about which way the Mexican went? Do you think he went north, or did he go back to Mexico?"

"If I go into the mountains to kill a deer, I stay until I kill a deer."

The answer made sense to Matt. If the Mexicans had come for gold, there didn't seem much reason for one of them to go home ahead of the rest of the group. "Your answer tells me you think he went north." Matt pointed. "Up that way. Why would he go up that way?"

"Maybe this Mexican has a map, too."

That wasn't it, Matt told himself. The Mexican would not go out on an independent search. "You know where the bell is located," said Matt. "If you wanted to get to the bell from where the Mexicans are camped, how would you travel . . . how would you get there?"

Cobre stirred at the coals with a stick. "Best way is to go to Madison's ranch. Come into mountains the way priest came."

Fourteen mounted men and twenty mules. If they went that way, trespassing, as it were, on Madison's land . . . drawing attention to themselves . . . they might very well tip their hand. Matt decided to approach it all from another direction. "If the Mexicans had a map of these mountains, and they could look at the map, would they see another way to reach the place where the bell is lying?"

"Cobre knows about maps," the Indian told Matt. "Soldiers show me how. When I was a scout, I went many places by looking at maps." Cobre scooted to a patch of open ground . . . drew a line with his fire-stirring stick.

Then he drew a small round circle on the line. "This is mountains," he said, indicating the line.

"Running south to north," said Matt.

"Yes. This is the big peak." He made another mark farther north. "This is the place where old mission once stood." He made another mark. "This is where Mexicans are camped. If Mexicans come same way we came . . . follow the tops of mountains . . . stay out of deep canyons, they can go up here." He pointed to the mark that indicated the location of the bell. "If a fire is built, at night, where the mission once stood, a man on top of mountains here"—he pointed with the stick—"could see fire below."

Matt nodded thoughtfully. What Cobre was saying—at least, what Matt felt he was saying—was that everyone associated with the Mexican expedition had a general idea of where the mission was once located. A map would have told them that. What they were waiting for, Matt surmised, was someone to pinpoint the location exactly. That, Matt told himself, would be the priest.

Matt sat in the darkness and thought about the priest. What if the priest was not a priest? What if the wealthy Mexican had put together a band of tough characters and sent them north for the gold? True, the priest had served the Sacraments to Juanita and her daughter. But . . . "Cobre," Matt said, "if we rise early and ride hard, how long will it take us to get back to Madison's ranch?"

"Nearly all of the day. Probably just before darkness . . . maybe sooner if we don't rest."

Matt leaned toward the place where Cobre had drawn in the dirt. He made a mark between the marks that indicated Madison's ranch and the Mexican camp. "When you watched the Mexican camp . . . before . . . when you were alone . . . did you see a Mexican ride out as we did today?"

Cobre shook his head. "No. Cobre see Mexican ride in, but no Mexican went out."

"Damn," said Matt softly. "I'd make a bet that each day a Mexican rides out and another Mexican rides in." He pointed to the mark he had made. "They have a spot up here somewhere. And they have one man that stays there, waiting for the priest to come out. They don't know when that will be, so they keep someone up there all the time. And they trade off."

Cobre, sitting in the flickering light of the small fire, nodded his agreement.

"Do you know where the closest fort is located? Where soldiers are stationed?"

"Tucson," said Cobre.

Again Matt cursed softly. "That's too far. Those Mexicans are in the country illegally. They could be arrested . . . deported."

"Shoot," said Cobre. "Better to shoot."

"Maybe," said Matt. "But we need some more men. There's four at the Circle M. . . . I don't know how many up at McNeal's place."

"This many," said Cobre, holding up nine fingers. Matt smiled. There was probably very little in the Altar Valley that Cobre did not know about.

"I would like to ride to Madison's ranch in the morning. Once we get there, we can talk about all this with Mrs. Madison and her foreman. I know that you're thinkin' about the priest. But the priest is still in the mountains. We can discuss him, too. Will you do that? I still want to know what happened to our friend, Cleve. The Mexicans and the priest might know. If we simply kill the priest and shoot the Mexicans, we might never find out."

Cobre thought about it for a few moments. Finally he nodded. "Tomorrow we will go to Madison's place."

While Matt lay between his blankets, waiting for sleep to come, a disturbing thought coursed through his mind. Two men were missing. Maybe two men were dead. Be careful, he told himself. Be careful.

At the Madison ranch Alicia and Pete rocked on the front porch. Pete, tired from the long ride back from McNeal's place, was resting his booted feet on the porch railing.

"I don't like it," said Alicia. "Truth to tell, I've been worried about Bob from the very start. But I was hoping that he would ride north in the mountains and then come out at McNeal's place. Now you tell me that nobody up that way has seen him."

"Nope. He didn't stop off at McNeal's for sure. I can see him gettin' separated from the padre. I can see him searchin' the mountains like you said. But I can't see him stayin' out this long."

"Pete," she said, her voice weary, "what can we do? What are you supposed to do when two people . . . people close to you . . . drop off the face of the earth?"

"I don't honestly know," Pete replied.

"Well," said Alicia, "one thing we can't do is sit and wring our hands. Things are getting caught up here. Tomorrow, we all go out. Tell the boys."

"Which way?" Pete wanted to know.

"We'll go north . . . fan out through the foothills and make a sweep up that way."

Pete rose from the rocker. He was getting weary, too. "I'll see you in the morning, Alicia."

In the heavy darkness of a canyon high in the Baboquivaris, the black-robed figure sat by a small fire. It was a fire built on open ground between soaring cliffs . . . a fire built five hundred and forty paces north of the place where he had found the bell. After more than a century the bell was half-buried under sand and rocks that had been washed down by the infrequent but often torrential rains. But it was there, and he had found it.

Not far from the fire there was a mound of newly removed dirt with a small prospector's pick resting on the top of the mound. The hole beside the pile of dirt was not a deep hole. He had dug only until the pick had struck the heavy planks. Then he brushed the dirt back to make certain that what he had struck was man-made. It was. Beams, each about six inches across . . . cemented together with hardened adobe mud. The secret storage vault of the mission of San Acacia del Norte.

# CHAPTER
## ★ 18 ★

For Matt the next day was a day of hard riding. They had a long way to go, and even though they stayed with the fairly level ground of the high ridges until noon, the way down the mountain was harder on Matt than the ride up. Matt had spent a major portion of his life in a saddle, but downhill riding always shook and jostled him.

They stopped once near another small spring. Matt had a feeling that Cobre knew every spring in the vast wilderness of the Baboquivaris. While they munched on the last scraps of food, Matt told himself that he was glad they were going into the ranch. He was sure that Cobre could survive on whatever grew in the canyons, but he doubted that he could. He looked across at Cobre and smiled. "You're a tough man, Cobre," he said.

Cobre, as usual, nodded.

"Why is that, I wonder?"

"I belong here . . . you white men belong where you came from."

Cobre, Matt told himself, not only made his feelings quite plain, but he repeated them whenever the opportunity arose. "I suspect you're right," he said.

● ● ●

While Matt and Cobre were taking their meal high in the Baboquivaris, Juanita and Theresa were busy with their routine of chores at the Madison ranch house. Juanita was in the kitchen, sliding pans of bread dough into the oven. Theresa was sweeping the long porch that ran the length of the house. When she reached the south end of the porch, she looked up and saw a mounted rider approaching from the west . . . coming out of the foothills at the base of the mountains. She quickly swept the debris off the end of the porch and hurried back into the house.

"Mama, Mama," she called from the front entrance. "Father Arredondo is returning." She continued on into the kitchen. Her mother closed the oven door, slowly wiped her hands on a cloth. She didn't seem to share her daughter's enthusiasm.

"I wish Señora Madison was here," Juanita said.

Theresa scowled just a little. "Mama, the priest is a good man. He would not forsake all things worldly if he was not truly a servant of God."

Juanita walked to her daughter and put an arm around her shoulder. "I am sure you are right, my child." But she didn't say it with a great deal of conviction. "Anyway, he will be hungry. We will prepare him some food."

Theresa saw him ride to the corral, dismount, and remove his gear from the horse. But he left the saddle and bridle on the animal. Then walked to the house.

He tapped gently on the sill of the opened back door. Juanita turned. "Ah, Father," she said, "please come in. Theresa saw you coming, and we have some food on the table."

"*Gracias*," replied the priest.

Juanita was anxious to know if the priest had seen young Bob. But obviously he hadn't, or the young man would have been with him. She followed him to the dining room. He sat and started eating without comment. She returned to the kitchen, poured a glass of water, and returned with it . . . set it on the table in front of him. "Did you have a good trip?" she asked.

"*Sí.*"

Juanita went back to the kitchen. Theresa spoke to her in a whisper. "May I go into the dining room and inquire about Bob?"

Her mother shook her head and waved a finger. "No. I want to see if he will mention it."

Several times Juanita went back to the dining room . . . taking food . . . removing things. Apparently, the priest was not in the mood for conversation. On her last trip Juanita asked, "Is there anything else I can bring you, Father?"

"No, señora," he said. "I'm going to ride out again. I am tired from my trek and would like to spend some time quietly in meditation. I'll return before darkness sets in."

The priest went briefly to his room, taking his bedroll and other gear with him. But in a matter of minutes he returned, thanked them for the meal, and went out the rear door.

Juanita and Theresa watched him go to the corral, mount up, and ride away.

"He did not mention young Bob . . . not one word," said Juanita. "I am going to stay out here, and I will watch constantly the direction in which he rode. I want you to go to his room. Look through everything."

"Mama, you frighten me," Theresa said. "I have never done such a thing . . . especially to a priest."

"You will find the courage to do it. Be careful. Note exactly where everything is lying . . . how everything is folded. Bring anything that you feel I should see out here. Especially, I want to see maps or anything written. Go do it now."

"Mama, I feel like I am doing something wrong."

"Very well," said Juanita. "I will tell you why I am concerned. When Father Arredondo prepared the Sacraments, he did not utter a single word of prayer. His lips moved silently, yes, and he had a familiarity with the procedure. But he did not hold his hands properly, and when he made the sign of the cross, he crossed from right to left." She paused for a moment to let the words sink in. "Eh? A priest that crosses himself in the wrong direction? I would have let it pass . . . never questioned it . . . never said a word.

But Bob is missing. Think about it, my daughter. Bob went into the mountains with the Father, and he did not come out. Now the Father does not even inquire . . . does not even ask if Bob returned."

Theresa was visibly shaken. "Mama, now I am truly frightened."

"Go," said Juanita. "I will keep a close watch." Obediently Theresa left the kitchen, went down the long hall of the house, and let herself into the priest's room.

Juanita went about her work, but every few minutes she glanced out the window watching the priest's path to the south.

When finally Theresa returned, she was carrying some items wrapped in a shawl. "Put it here," said Juanita, gesturing toward a kitchen table. Theresa did as her mother commanded. Before crossing to the table, Juanita took a long look out the window. Then she approached Theresa.

"Mama," Theresa said. "I did not bring the big pistols. There were two of them in holsters . . . a belt with cartridges, also."

Juanita nodded. "That would not be unusual. He might have worn them under the robe. A man going into wild country might well wear pistols . . . even if he was a priest." She made a motion with her hand, telling Theresa to open the bundle.

Theresa folded back the cloth. There were four items in the shawl. Juanita scowled. She reached out and picked up one of the two small weapons. Although Juanita could not have identified them by name, they were a matched pair of Remington 41-caliber, over and under pistols . . . each small enough to be concealed in the hand . . . or in a pocket. She looked at Theresa. "He has a rifle which he carries on his saddle and two big pistols which, apparently, he wears under his robe. Hmm."

Theresa pointed. "And look at that, Mama."

Juanita *did* look. Then she reached out and picked up the scabbard from the table . . . took hold of the bone handle and slowly withdrew the implement from the sheath. She looked at it for a long time . . . turned it in her hand. She held it up, close to her face, and examined it. "A man in the wilderness would have good use for a sharp knife . . . a knife to clean game with . . . a knife to do other things." She slid her hand along the blade. "But this is not a knife for common work. It is not sharp enough to cut with." She touched her finger to the tip. "This knife was made for only one thing. This knife was made to be plunged into another man. This is a dagger!"

Carefully she raised her apron and wiped the blade, then slid the eight-inch dagger back in the scabbard. "Those pistols are the kind that gamblers carry . . . hidden in a boot or someplace else."

"Maybe he is a fearful man," Theresa offered.

"Sweet Father Kino, who wandered this land all his life, never carried a weapon. I know that to be true. Priests put their lives in God's hands. Perhaps a priest would carry a rifle into bad country. Maybe even a pair of pistols. But . . ." She looked distastefully at the weapons lying on the cloth.

Theresa reached out and picked up the final item . . . a roll wrapped and bound by a thin cord. "I read some of this," she said as she untied the roll. Juanita stepped to the window and looked to the south . . . then hurried back and took a chair.

Theresa removed some sheets with handwriting, smoothed the largest document, and bent over it. Juanita, who could not read, leaned closer. "Tell me what it says."

"This map is a map of the mountains. It is an old map, eh? But some of the writing is new." She pointed. "This writing is new, as is the square box drawn here. It says 'ranch.' Over here is Tubac. Up here, another box drawn. It also says 'ranch.' I think, Mama, that this is our ranch . . . this is Señor McNeal's ranch."

Juanita studied the map and nodded. "These lines are a trail, *sí?*"

"I think so, Mama."

Juanita pursed her lips. "This is the kind of a map the priest would carry. What else?"

Theresa drew out another map and spread it in front of Juanita. "This map is a map showing the old mission. Only one thing that is new has been placed on this map."

Juanita's finger went immediately to the place where the ink was darker . . . fresher by many years than the other notations on the map. "This," she said, pointing to a three-letter word and a coarsely drawn arrow. "I know this word. *Oro* . . . gold." She looked up at Theresa. "So. Remember the story that José told us the other night at the dinner table . . . about the buried gold of San Acacia del Norte?"

"Yes, Mama," Theresa replied.

"Why would the priest write the word *gold* on the map if he was only looking for the old site so a monument could be built there?"

"There is more, Mama." She picked up the sheaf of handwritten sheets. "I read through this in the priest's room. Everything on these sheets is about gold. It speaks of a bell . . . of an underground vault. There is something here . . ." She leafed through the pages. "Something about the amounts of gold and silver. Listen, Mama . . . 650 large bars of gold . . . 338 small bars of gold . . . 222 bars of silver. There is more listed here."

Juanita wrinkled her brow. "If there is gold there, then the gold belongs to the church. He would have a right to keep it a secret . . . to tell a small lie. But . . ."

"You think it is all right, then?" asked Theresa. "He *is* a good man of God, no?"

"A good man of God knows how to make the sign of the cross, my daughter. And what of that?" she said, pointing to the weapons.

"I don't know, Mama."

Juanita repeated herself. "A priest who does not know how to cross himself . . . who does not know how to hold his hands during the preparation of the Sacraments . . . who does not inquire about a young man who has been missing for many days. And he carries a dagger and a pair of gambler's pistols."

"Do you think he is a bad priest?" asked Theresa.

"I do not think he is a priest at all," replied Juanita. She pointed to the maps and the written sheets. "Fold those exactly as they were and tie the cord around them. Put everything back exactly where you found it. Do it now."

Theresa complied obediently. She moved down the hall toward the priest's room. Juanita looked out the window again, then stood at the sill . . . deep in thought. She hoped that Alicia and the others would return before Father Arredondo. She needed to talk to Alicia.

Four miles south of the ranch house Father Arredondo sat on the ground in the shade of a large mesquite tree. The short Mexican with one blind eye and a drooping mustache was bent over a map . . . an exact copy of the large map that Theresa had shown her mother. Arredondo, holding a small sharp twig, moved the twig on a line that had previously been drawn along the high ridges. He stopped at a certain point and punched a small hole in the paper. Speaking in Spanish, he told the Mexican, "Be at this place before nightfall tomorrow. Place men out a half mile apart north and south of this point. As soon as the mountains are in total darkness, watch for the light of a fire. Every man will keep a sharp lookout. The fire will burn for only a short time. So . . . the man who sees it must mark the location well in his mind. That man will call out, and the call will be passed along the line. Rendezvous with the man who has spotted the fire. By the light of early morning you will be able to see the small valley. I will be waiting. Tell the others that I dug with my pick and uncovered the beams. The gold is there, Miguel . . . the gold is there."

A broad smile spread across Miguel's ugly countenance.

# CHAPTER

## ★ 19 ★

It was late in the afternoon when Juanita scurried out of the kitchen and made her way to Alicia's living quarters. There, Theresa was dusting furniture. "He's riding in," said Juanita. "You come to the kitchen and stay there. Besides, it is nearly time to set the dinner table."

Theresa followed her mother back to the kitchen, where curiosity prompted her to look out the window . . . to watch as the robed figure guided his horse to the corral. This time he removed the saddle and bridle, then walked back to the house. As before, he tapped on the door, then let himself in. "Ah, Father," said Juanita, "I'm sure the others will return soon, and we will have a nice meal."

"Bueno," he replied . . . then turned and left the room.

Juanita walked to the kitchen door, casually watching until Father Arredondo let himself into his room at the far end of the hall. Then she hurried back to the kitchen and drew close to the counter where Theresa was working. "Have you noticed, my daughter, that when he first arrived how courteous and polished he appeared? No longer. He is not friendly at all."

"*Sí*," said Theresa. "He did not even greet me . . . not even say 'good day.' "

"Well . . . we must prepare dinner as usual. And when Pete and Alicia return, I will speak to them about all of this."

• • •

In the room Arredondo sat on the edge of the bed. He was tired. This gold hunting was hard work . . . not very much to his liking. But the reward would be substantial. More than substantial. He would receive a handsome share from his patron, Juan Antonio Diaz. Probably the share would be enough to live on comfortably for many years. On the other hand, Señor Diaz might not fully appreciate the tiring labor he had performed . . . the skills of his quick mind that were critical to the success of the endeavor . . .nor the risks he had faced. In order to make sure that he was not shortchanged by his patron, he had made a side deal with two of the other members of the party. It was a simple plan that would be easy to carry out. It merely involved a little cooperation among the three of them behind the backs of the others. Put very simply, they would hide thirty gold bars along the trail back to Mexico and return later. However, there was another plan to be laid on top of that plan. When, at some later date, the three of them rode north to pick up the hidden thirty bars, he would dispatch his companions with bullets to the head and claim the entire prize. He had observed, at a very early age, that life is tough, and he had always subscribed to a belief that it takes a tough man to find his way successfully through the difficult ordeal of life.

He took a long breath and let it out. He was, indeed, very tired. A short siesta before dinner seemed in order, but first he wanted to check a detail or two on one of the maps. He went to his knees by the bed, reached under it, and pulled out his bedroll and other gear. He acquired the roll of maps with the old pages from the church archives inside . . . rose to his feet and walked across the room to a table . . . pulled out the chair and sat down. He started to reach for the cord that bound the roll . . . then stopped . . . his fingers suspended in midair. Slowly he lowered his hand, laid the roll on the table, and intently eyed the cord.

Francisco Diego Castenada (for that was his real name) had, during the thirty-one years of his life, killed six men with pistols and two with knives . . . another he had beaten to death with a large rock. For all of his mature years he had lived outside the law. Such men do not tie bows.

The cord wrapped around the roll was, as he observed, tied in a small, neat bow. He reached out and loosened the bow . . . then unrolled the maps. He looked at everything carefully. Then he rose and returned to his belongings on the floor by the bed. Meticulously he went through them. On the grip of one of the small pistols he noticed a small, white speck. He removed it with his fingers . . . held it in front of his face and examined it. Then he pressed the speck between his fingers and rubbed the fingers together. Afterward he held them to his nose. The smell was, unmistakably, that of fresh bread dough.

Less than thirty minutes after the robed Castenada had gone to the privacy of his room, Alicia, Pete, and the two Mexican cowboys returned to the house. Juanita heard them riding up at the front, and she hurried to the door, opened it, and greeted them.

"Anybody else here?" Alicia asked as she slid from her mount.

"Sí, señora, the good priest is back." Juanita smiled broadly.

Alicia turned to Pete. "Pete, I'm a tired woman. Will you take my horse down and let me go on in?"

Before Pete could answer, Juanita was excitedly motioning with her hand. The smile was no longer on her face. Alicia looked at her quizzically. Juanita continued to motion, obviously urging them to enter the house immediately.

Alicia, with a strange look on her face, turned to Pete. "On second thought, tie them all here, and we'll go in and have something to drink first."

Alicia was the first up the steps, Pete and the cowboys close behind. Juanita hurried ahead of them into the kitchen. She motioned to Theresa to watch the front of the house from the door. Then she ushered Alicia and the others to the far side of the room.

"What's wrong?" asked Alicia. Juanita told her. Told her everything she had observed in the priest's behavior . . . told her about the dagger, the tiny pistols, and the map and the written pages. Told her how the supposed priest had not inquired about the missing Bob Whipple. When Juanita had finished, Alicia turned to Pete. "I want to talk to that man, right now."

"I think that's a good idea," he said.

Alicia pointed to his holstered pistol. "I trust that's loaded." He nodded that it was. "Let's go, then."

The two of them left the room, Alicia in the lead. She stopped at the priest's room . . . knocked. No answer. She knocked again . . . more loudly. Still no answer. Alicia called out. "Father!" She waited a moment. "Father!" She pointed to Pete's pistol. He drew it out slowly. Alicia stepped back, and Pete turned the knob and opened the door.

The room was empty. Pete gestured toward the window . . . the shutters were standing open . . . a breeze blowing through. "All of his belongings are gone, too."

They hurried out . . . back to the kitchen. "He's not here," Alicia told the others. "Pete, I want you and Manuel to go down to the corral and see if he's ridden off." A disturbing thought had taken a foremost position in her mind. Cleve was missing. Bob was missing. Matt wasn't back. Matt was supposed to stay behind the priest, but still . . . "Be careful," she cautioned. Pete nodded and he and Manuel went out the back door.

Alicia looked at the others in the room. "Very good work, Juanita . . . Theresa . . . very good." Then her eyes went to José. "I don't think he's anywhere else in the house, but I want you to take your pistol and check all the other rooms."

"*Sí*, señora," José said. He removed his weapon from its holster and started down the hall.

"Let me have a cup of coffee," said Alicia. Immediately young Theresa poured for her. Then Alicia walked to the dining room and sat at the table.

Castenada had seen the riders come in. He made a face, angry at himself that he had not moved with greater speed.

He needed to leave and leave quickly. Surely the fat old bag with bread dough on her hands would give them all a briefing.

He watched the activity from a hidden position behind one of the outbuildings . . . the large one standing next to the corral. He moved quickly to an opened door and stepped inside . . . placed his bedroll and other items on a stack of grain bags. He strapped the gunbelt around his waist . . . the dagger went into his boot. He had no real desire for violence. Not now, anyway. What he really wanted to do was to get away from the ranch . . . get some much-needed rest and prepare himself for another difficult trip into the Baboquivaris.

When he had checked his pistols, making sure that both were fully loaded, he stepped back outside . . . started for the corner of the building.

Noises carry in the quiet desert air, and he heard the slam of a door at the house . . . the sound of heavy bootheels on the porch. He sneaked a look around the corner. He saw Pete and Manuel coming his way.

When they got to the corral and saw his horse, they would know he hadn't left. That's what Castenada told himself. It wouldn't do to shoot them. Another cowboy was up at the house, and he was certain that Alicia knew how to use a weapon. He had noticed, of course, the rack of rifles hanging in the dining area.

If he did shoot the two coming his way, he would then have to saddle and bridle his horse. By that time those in the house would have time to prepare. Safe behind the heavy adobe walls and armed with rifles, they could pick him off as he rode away. No, he told himself . . . it would be much better if it were all done quietly.

Then there was the Texan . . . Ramsey. Castenada wondered where he was. Suddenly an idea impacted Castenada's mind. That's the way it had always been for him . . . he was a man of good intellect and good ideas. That's why he had survived so long . . . why Señor Diaz had chosen him for this special job. Just killing off the two men approaching the corral would not be enough. After that others might try to pursue him . . . the woman and the other cowboy . . .the Texan, too, if he returned soon. Someone might even ride north to the neighboring ranch for help. Castenada told himself that he needed protection. Even with the sound of approaching footsteps, Castenada smiled. That's the way he was . . . a man with an almost suicidal proclivity for violence and for danger. "*Muy loco*," was the way one of his long-term acquaintances once put it. So loco, in fact, that many of his associates in Mexico feared him.

Castenada slipped into the building . . . looked about. The large room, piled with grain bags and implements of various kinds, was not really suited for an ambush. Oh, well, he told himself . . . why not keep it simple? He stood inside the door, back pressed to the wall, and waited. Simple was often best, he told himself as he slipped the sharp dagger out of his boot. With the left hand he drew one of the pistols and laid it on a grain bag. Waited. He could hear them by the corral now.

"Well," said Pete's voice, "he ain't rode out . . . not with his horse still here."

"You want me to go look over there?" said Manuel's voice.

"Do that," replied Pete. "I'll go down and check around the Indian huts."

Castenada waited. He could hear approaching footsteps . . . only one set of footsteps.

Manuel Garza was a bright man, but he was human enough that the image of a priest remained in his mind. Even though he had absorbed all that Juanita said in the kitchen, he still saw the man he was looking for as a priest. That was how he had seen him on every occasion before . . . a somber, quiet man in a long black robe. Priests, of course, were not generally thought of as dangerous . . . or even as strong. Manuel approached the outbuilding and stepped into the doorway without even drawing his pistol. Probably it would not have made any difference if he had. From the shadows beside the stack of grain bags, Castenada took one step and slammed the dagger into Manuel's stomach with such force that he was nearly lifted from his feet. As the cowboy slumped, Castenada twisted the tip upward, and it found Manuel's heart.

Juanita had been right about the small pistols. She had said they were carried by gamblers. Castenada *was* a gambler . . . a gambler in everything he did. So instead of hiding Manuel's body, he did exactly the opposite. He dragged it out of the door and laid it on the ground, facedown . . . just outside.

Then Castenada slipped back inside and again took a position in the near-darkness by the grain bags.

Several minutes passed. Then Pete called Manuel's name. Again silence. Then the sound of footsteps. "Let's go back up to the house," Pete called. Castenada waited calmly. He had confidence in his simple plan.

Now the footsteps were just around the corner off the building. Castenada strained his ears. Now they were *at* the corner. Suddenly they stopped. The sound was very low in Pete's throat, but Castenada heard it . . . just a soft moan. Then more steps. Castenada could see the body on the ground. He could also see Pete as he bent down and touched the fallen cowboy. Simple plans are best, Castenada thought once more as he lunged through the door and came down on Pete . . . the dagger going in right between the foreman's shoulder blades, just to the right of the spine.

Castenada was pleased. It had all been simple, swift, and silent. He retrieved his pistol and stood quietly . . . thinking. If he went around the far side of the outbuilding, he could approach the house from the end where the cowboys bunked. That way he would not be seen coming from the corral.

Castenada moved quickly but as silently as possible. When he reached the house, he removed his boots . . . stepped onto the long wooden porch. Moved toward the kitchen door. Stepped inside with pistol drawn.

Juanita gasped when she saw him. Theresa, holding a pan of water, froze . . . petrified with fear. Fear was often a valuable ally. He glared at the two women . . . thrust the pistol forward so they could see the long barrel. Then he raised a finger to his lips . . . the sign for silence. He knew that he had only seconds and parts of seconds before one of them broke out of the spell and screamed.

Castenada . . . moving quickly . . . made it to the dining room. Alicia looked up. She, too, was momentarily frozen by the sight of the armed man pointing a weapon in her direction. But it was only for an instant. She rose from the table and at the same time called out, "Juanita! Out of the house! Now!"

The sounds of frantic scrambling could be heard in the kitchen . . . the banging of the door thrown outward so hard it hit the adobe wall.

Alicia glanced to the wall where a half dozen rifles were resting in an open gun rack. "Hsst!" said Castenada. She dared not move.

Castenada was good at his business, and sometimes his business required counting. He knew that there were three cowboys. Two were dead . . . so one remained. He slid across the room, pressed his back to the wall . . . all the time watching Alicia. He edged toward the alcove that opened to the large living room and the hall beyond.

He heard footsteps on the wooden floor of the hall. Alicia called out, "José . . . stay back!"

No time to waste, Castenada told himself. He stepped into the alcove. José had his pistol in his hand, but José was a cowboy, not a gunfighter. Astonishment made him slow to react. Castenada's pistol barked once, and José Escobar, hit full in the chest, flew back against a wall and slid down it to the floor, leaving a long and ugly streak of blood on the white stucco.

Castenada whirled. Alicia had her hands on one of the rifles. As she lifted, Castenada leaped across the room and brought the barrel of the pistol down on Alicia's arm with such force that she went to her knees in pain. Castenada stood over her . . . relaxed now. The job was done. He gave her a few moments, not out of benevolence but because he knew that she probably would not be able to stand until the pain abated.

Moments passed. "Stand up," he said. Alicia complied, holding her arm as she did. Her face reflected a great deal of pain. "Listen carefully," said Castenada. "If I so desired, I could slice your throat without a shred of remorse. So." He backed off a step or two. "You are going to ride with me. If you cause me no trouble, I will later release you. If you *do* cause me trouble, I will kill you. *Comprende?*"

She nodded.

"We will go out the front way." He motioned with the pistol. Once on the porch he told her, "Take your horse and walk him to the corral. *Andale!*"

Castenada took them around the house and retrieved his boots. As they walked to the corral, Castenada saw a flash of color move between two of the small adobe huts where the Indian workers had formerly lived. Either the young girl or the old bag . . . no problem, he told himself.

At the corral he kept a close eye on Alicia while he saddled his mount. "That way," he said, pointing to the outbuilding. She walked ahead of him, leading her mount. When they turned the corner of the building, she momentarily recoiled at the sight of Pete and Manuel lying bloody in the dirt. Castenada edged around the bodies . . . keeping an eye on Alicia. He went through the door, scooped up his bedroll, and quickly stepped back out. "On your horse," he said.

Alicia did as ordered. "Leave the women alone. Both you and I know where they're hiding. I won't ride down that way. If you want me to go with you, you must leave them alone."

Castenada chuckled. "What do I want with them?" He motioned with the pistol. "Go in that direction."

"Into the mountains?"

"*Sí*, señora. We are going into the mountains to feast our eyes on something that no man has seen for more than one hundred years . . . the gold of San Acacia del Norte."

# CHAPTER
## ★ 20 ★

In full darkness Matt and Cobre rode the lowest foothills of the Baboquivaris, angling toward the broad sweep of Altar Valley. The twisting route they had taken had confused Matt. He wasn't sure just exactly where they were relative to the ranch. At one point he stopped his horse. "Cobre," he called. "How far to the ranch house."

Cobre pointed. "Out there."

Matt looked but saw nothing. Part of a moon remained, but Matt could see nothing that was recognizable. "How far?"

"Two miles . . . no more than that."

Again Matt strained his eyes. He had ridden into the ranch in darkness a number of times with Alicia. Something was different . . . something was not as it should be. There were no pinpoints of light in the distance. "Can you see the house from here?" Matt inquired.

"Yes," said Cobre.

"Then I should be able to see lights, but I don't." Surely they hadn't retired so early, Matt told himself. And just as sure, all of them would not be away from the ranch at this hour. "There should be some light out there. The darkness tells me that no one's there . . . or something else."

"We see," Cobre replied, shaking the reins and urging his steed on down the incline.

Matt was damn near exhausted, and the horses were tired. He didn't know about Cobre. But bushed or not, Matt felt a sense of urgency. When they hit flat ground, Matt let the horse break into a gallop. The animal knew that they were on the last leg home, and even though tired, it was willing to run toward water and feed. Cobre stayed at Matt's side.

When they were close enough for Matt to recognize the dark outline of the house, he slowed his pace . . . finally pulled the buckskin to a halt. "I don't like what I see up there," Matt said. "There should be some lights in the house. Let's move quietly and see what's up."

"You and horses stay here," Cobre replied. "I take look." Even before Matt could answer, the Indian was off his horse. He passed the reins to Matt, then slipped into the darkness.

Matt sat in the saddle and waited. He could sense the trouble that had lately enveloped the Circle M Ranch. When he had first arrived in the Altar Valley, it was only that Cleve was missing. That had been enough. But over a period of time more trouble had rolled in until it lay across the valley like a mist. Now Matt could feel it all around him. All of the pieces added up to an ugly whole.

Matt kept telling himself that the waiting wasn't nearly as long as it seemed to be. Except for a few night-calling birds and, once, the distant wail of a coyote, the valley was ominously quiet.

The horses were as restless as Matt. Not long ago they had been bolting for the corral, where they would find rest and sustenance. Cobre's horse was especially impatient. It danced, whinnied . . . pulled against the reins. Matt was trying to settle the animal when, without a sound, Cobre appeared under the horse's neck. He took the reins and leaped into the saddle . . . pointed to the west. "We go tie horses . . . walk in. No people . . . no sound."

As they rode toward a small grove of mesquite trees, Matt felt a sick sensation welling up inside him. They tied the horses in amongst the trees . . . then, with Cobre leading, moved toward the house at a trot.

They came in on the south side. Cobre stopped after they reached the wall of the house. With hand signals and a few whispered words, he laid out a simple strategy. Both of them would edge along the porch . . . Cobre would go in alone. They slid along the wall, went up on the porch, and moved carefully to the front door. Cobre let himself in. Matt waited . . . his rifle at the ready.

Again Cobre's absence seemed a long one. Finally he emerged. He leaned close to Matt and whispered. "One man dead inside."

"No one else."

"No," Cobre replied. He pointed to the corral and outbuildings. "I go down there. You stay here." Matt nodded.

Waiting in the darkness was not Matt's cup of tea. Fear for Alicia and the others was starting to mix with the general feeling of doom that had arrived earlier.

Again, Cobre returned soundlessly. "Two more men dead down there." Now the feelings of fear and doom rolled like thunder over Matt. Without consulting Cobre, he made a hasty judgment. Something intuitive told him that the killer—or killers—were not on the property.

Matt shouted out, "Alicia!" Silence. "Alicia! It's Matt!"

Still silence. Then, from the area of the Indian huts, a woman's voice called back. "Señor Ramsey!"

"Let's go," said Matt. He was off the porch and running, Cobre at his side.

They found Juanita and Theresa quaking at the corner of one of the small adobe structures. Theresa looked as though she was in shock. Juanita was wringing her hands. "Señor Ramsey . . . it was horrible. Shooting. He took Alicia away."

"Who?" asked Matt.

"The man in the black robe. He is no priest. He is an evil man."

Matt was experiencing a terrible sinking feeling. Sonofabitch, he cursed silently. Cobre had been right. He should have let the Indian kill the bastard in the mountains. Matt looked at Cobre, then back at Juanita. "Did they leave on horses?"

"*Sí*. We could see them as they rode away."

"He's taken her as a hostage," said Matt. "Damn!" He looked back at Cobre. "Can you track in this light?"

"Not in rocks . . . not at night."

"Could you tell what direction they went when they left here? We need to know where they're headed."

"Ramsey," Cobre said, "remember what I told you about the crazy gold. The black robe is on his way to the place of the bell. Is that not so?"

Matt realized something. There was a truth he needed to face. When it came to hunting men, Cobre was his superior. That was an undeniable fact, Matt told himself. From this point on he would rely on Cobre's experience and instinct. He turned to Juanita. "Just one man . . . was that all?"

"*Sí*, señor . . . just one."

"Cobre and I will follow them. There is a dead man inside the house. I don't know who. And there are two more outside." Juanita gasped. "I'm sorry that we have to leave you with somethin' like that."

Juanita made the sign of the cross. Theresa did likewise.

"We need your help . . . right now. You gotta go in the house and pull some food together for us." He turned to Cobre. "Is the body in the kitchen?"

"No," said Cobre. "In room where people sit to eat."

"Cobre and I will move the body outside . . . take it to the out-building where the others are located. We'll wrap them in blankets and put them inside. Tomorrow morning you and Theresa need to start digging graves. I'm sorry, Juanita, but we must leave right away."

"I understand, Señor Ramsey. Please bring Señora Madison back safely. That is what I pray."

Matt, of course, had known who the dead men would be. There had never been any doubt about that. But actually seeing them . . . lifting them . . . getting their blood on his hands and clothes was a sad and sobering experience. No matter how many dead men you see, Matt told himself, you never truly get used to it.

In less than thirty minutes Juanita had their food items ready and Matt had filled his water flasks. Then he removed a pair of rifles from the rack in the dining room . . . made sure that both were loaded. He presented the weapons to Juanita. "I am sure," Matt told her, "that the priest . . . or whoever he is . . . won't be back here. But I think it will make you feel better if you keep these with you. Lock the door to your room and bar the shutters." Juanita accepted the weapons and assured Matt that they would start digging the first thing in the morning.

Matt and Cobre left the two women and went to the corral . . . saddled up the horses and rode away into the night.

At the base of the foothills Matt stopped . . . surveyed the dark mass of land that heaved itself up in front of him. It had been bad country in daylight, but at night . . . "Cobre," he asked, "do you think that the priest can continue to travel through the night?"

"No," Cobre told him. "He will not even try. Remember, Ramsey, he is not Apache. He needs rest. You need rest, too. Horses need rest. Eh?"

Matt had to agree with him. Matt knew that he could not ride through the night. But if it were possible to close the gap and overtake the priest, he would make the try. "Could you find their trail?"

"We passed the trail . . . crossed it way back there." Cobre pointed. "Cobre knows better way. We go that way."

"Can we catch up with them tomorrow?"

Cobre shrugged his shoulders. "Don't know how far black robe is ahead of us. Señora Montoya said they went in daylight, but how far ahead, Cobre doesn't know."

"Do you think he will get to the old mission tomorrow?"

"He could reach place of the bell by end of day tomorrow. No sooner."

"And when can we get there?"

Cobre did not answer him directly. "Remember, Ramsey, other Mexicans will be coming, too. Don't know when. We could get there at night, but too much darkness in canyon. We can't see."

Matt realized that even Cobre had his limitations. He knew what the former scout was saying. It would endanger Alicia, and their own lives as well, if they stumbled into a confined area with fourteen or fifteen armed adversaries.

"No campfires . . . Mexicans make no campfire," Cobre said.

Matt realized that, too. The priest anticipated pursuit. That's why he had taken Alicia with him. There would be no campfires . . . and quite possibly, if the other Mexicans arrived, armed guards waiting along the trail. "What should we do?" he asked Cobre.

Cobre pointed to the dark bulk of mountain, aiming his finger at some indistinct point high in the foothills. "We ride up there now. We sleep until first light. Then go on."

"All right," said Matt.

Sixteen miles northwest of the place where Matt and Cobre stopped for the night and two thousand feet higher in elevation, Castenada rested on a large rock. Eight feet away, her hands trussed in front of her, Alicia sat on the hard earth contemplating her captor.

"This is where we stay for the night," said Castenada. "I have only two blankets, and it will get cold before morning. But I have a great deal of respect for women . . . so I am going to give you one of the blankets. But . . . I cannot give you any food. The only food I have is just a few crumbs left in my saddlebags. I need my strength, señora. You understand that, I'm sure."

He went to his horse and removed a length of rawhide rope. "You would die if you ran away in these mountains. For your own good I must tie your legs. Not tightly," he said as he knelt down at her feet. "Just a hobble, like we put on our horses, eh?"

"Do you know anything about my husband?" she asked.

"You have a husband?"

"Yes."

"But he was not one of the men at the ranch . . . the men who tried to interfere today . . . eh?"

"No. He's been missing for many days. Maybe . . ." Her arm was throbbing . . . she was consumed by fatigue . . . she was frightened. She was having trouble remembering. "Maybe three weeks."

Castenada finished the hobble and stood up. He chuckled. "Three weeks is not so long. Sometimes a man gets to drinking with friends . . . meets a nice lady someplace." He laughed "Time flies by, if you know what I mean."

"You can have the damn gold," she told him. "All of this violence was unnecessary. I just want my husband back."

"Where is the man from Texas?" he asked abruptly.

Alicia thought about it. What should she tell him? She didn't know for sure where Matt was. But the question meant that Arredondo, or whoever he was, didn't know, either. Most likely Matt was alive . . . but where?

"Eh?"

"He left. He was just passing through . . . visiting."

The priest tossed a blanket to her. "You stay right there. Don't get up."

"Could I have a drink of water?"

"We don't have much water, also. I'll give you a drink in the morning."

"If I could just have a little . . . one mouthful."

Castenada pulled the blanket around his shoulders. "You boss people around a lot, don't you?" he said. "You boss those two women around . . . you bossed those cowboys around. Don't boss me around. Shut up and go to sleep."

# CHAPTER

# ⋆21⋆

Matt slept poorly. It was not the hard ground, but rather thoughts of Alicia and her dangerous situation that made sleep so difficult. He was awake when Cobre stirred and rolled out of his tattered blanket.

They ate a few bites of cold food, saddled the horses, and started on. "We can't reach the old mission today . . . isn't that what you told me?" asked Matt as they rode.

"We will go to the deep canyon north of place where the mission once stood. It will be dark by then. We sleep . . . then next day at first light we go to top of ridge. Look down. We see things. How many men . . . where they are . . . what they are doing. Then Cobre will tell you what to do."

Matt was satisfied to let Cobre make the plan. He rode behind the Indian mile after tortuous uphill mile. Tomorrow morning, regardless of how it all worked out, the whole thing would come to some sort of an end. Cobre was right. Gold *did* make men crazy. Probably Cleve was as dead as the cowboys back at the ranch. Bob Whipple, too. Five good, decent men. All because some blackhearted bastard down in Mexico . . . a man he had never seen, whose name he did not know . . . a man already wealthy, wanted something that didn't belong to him.

And what of the fake priest? Matt had known men like

him in the past. Scum, he told himself. The worst of a mongrel breed. Matt made a promise to himself. The black robe, as Cobre called him, had already received his sentence of death. If he had to travel to Mexico and dog the man's tracks forever, Matt promised himself that he would avenge those whose lives had been ripped and torn by the callous killer.

The day was a day of consummate monotony. Swaying in the saddle. Following the Indian in and out of twisted gorges . . . over rocky ridges . . . through brush-choked arroyos. The only indication to Matt that it would eventually end was the movement of the sun and the changing shadows. Night *would* eventually come. And tomorrow morning—if all went well—he would put the false priest in his sights and send him to the hell he deserved.

They were less than a thousand feet below the crest in fast-fading light when Cobre stopped and slid from his horse. He pointed toward the south. "Over there is the valley where the bell rests in the deep arroyo. We will camp here. No fire. We will go over the top of the mountain as soon as daylight comes."

Matt's emotions told him to climb to the top of the ridge and look down now. But his logical mind told him that it would be pitch black by the time he ascended to the summit. He looked at Cobre. The Indian's face showed no emotion at all. Matt wanted to make sure that Cobre understood the priorities. "Cobre, rescuing the woman is the most important thing. Most important. We must do everything to save the woman."

Cobre said nothing for a few moments. Then that tiny hint of a smile showed at the corner of his mouth. "Ramsey, why do you think we climbed these mountains all day? I don't have to work this hard to kill the black robe and the Mexicans. I could sleep all day in the valley and wait for them to come out of the mountains."

"Thanks," said Matt.

A more serious look came over Cobre's face. "Do you like to go into battle, Ramsey?"

"I've been in some. Big battles where many men were

killed and wounded. No, Cobre, I don't like going into battle."

"I like going into battle," said Cobre. "It is my nature."

The statement, spoken matter-of-factly and without emotion, sent a shiver up Matt's spine, and he remembered that Cobre, single-handedly, had killed two squads of American cavalry, except for the one that had managed to dash into the agency. No doubt about it, Matt told himself . . . Cobre *was* suited to warfare. It *was* his nature.

The gentle tapping on Matt's shoulder brought him out of a troubling dream. He opened his eyes. Cobre was kneeling at his side. The sun was up! He heaved himself to a sitting position. Cobre spoke softly. "I have been to the ridge . . . looked down into the valley. The black robe is there. Madison's squaw is there. The Mexicans are on the old trail and coming down from above."

"Why didn't you wake me?" Matt asked.

"I went in darkness."

Matt threw the blankets aside and slipped on his boots. "Can we get there before the Mexicans?"

"No," said Cobre. "Mexicans will be there. You shoot Mexicans, I will get Madison's squaw."

"You already got that figured?"

"Yes," said Cobre. "When we get to top of ridge and can look down, I will tell you my plan."

Within five minutes they were on their horses and laboring up the last steep ridge. Matt filled his jacket pockets with ammunition for the rifle . . . checked his pistol to make sure that it was fully loaded. After that he closed his eyes for a few moments. It was a short and silent prayer for Alicia's rescue . . . no more than that.

A few yards below the ridge, at a place where a gnarled and ancient juniper tree grew in the rocky soil, Cobre stopped and dismounted . . . tied his horse. Matt did the same. Then he followed the Apache up through the tangle of boulders.

Cobre slid along the point of the ridge, bent low. Matt did the same. The Indian worked his way into a small, brushy draw, then went to the ground and crawled around a jutting shelf of rock. He signaled with his hand for Matt to come forward and join him.

They were lying on their bellies, elbow to elbow. Cobre pointed, and Matt stretched his neck and looked down into the canyon. Less than a hundred yards below was the relatively level surface of a tiny valley. It seemed that men and animals were everywhere. The mules were there . . . horses, too . . . and Mexicans. Men moving about, intent on their work. Seven or eight were digging . . . the rest doing other chores.

On the far side of the valley there was a cliff, its base eroded by eons of rushing water that roared through the canyon every time it rained in the higher regions. The erosion had carved back into the rock, creating a protective overhang. Back in the shadows, hands tied in front of her, was Alicia. Just outside the dark shadowed area, a man . . . a guard . . . sat on a large boulder, his legs crossed, rifle across his lap. He was leisurely smoking.

The noise of picks and shovels clanging against rock and loose soil filled the canyon. Cobre pointed back toward the brushy draw from which they had recently emerged. "Go downhill . . . that way." Matt nodded. Cobre pointed toward another shelf of rock down the canyon. "Crawl out of arroyo and get on big rock . . . wait there."

"You goin' for Alicia?"

Cobre pointed across the valley to the top of the cliff. "Cobre come out up there. Don't shoot. I will make signal with knife. You watch for flash of sunlight. Still don't shoot. When I kill guard . . . then you shoot. You shoot good?"

"I shoot pretty good."

Cobre was gone. Matt watched the activity for a few moments, then slid back into the brushy draw and started downhill. He came out at the spot indicated by Cobre . . . slithered along on his belly and put himself in a position to fire down on the Mexicans. He had heard some men say that tradition—or maybe it was frontier ethics—had it that you never fire on a man without giving him fair chance to defend himself. War had washed that silly idea from Matt's mind long ago. He and Cobre were badly outnumbered, and fairness was not the issue here, Matt told himself. The element of surprise was the advantage he needed, and Matt intended to use the advantage in the most deadly way possible.

Matt watched the surrounding terrain as well as the valley. He was trying to catch a glimpse of Cobre, but the Indian never showed himself . . . not even for a fleeting instant. It was a long way around to the other side of the valley, so Matt tried, as best he could, to relax, but his heart was thumping in his chest. He could feel the sweat building up under his shirt. He wiped some of it from the palms of his hands.

He watched the Mexicans, busy at their digging. Suddenly he heard a voice below yelling. *"Palos . . . palos!!"* Other voices, joined in exuberently. *"Hurra! Hurra!"* Mexicans were clapping their hands . . . some whistling loudly. *"El techo!"* shouted another. Matt had no trouble understanding what was going on below. The Mexicans had hit wood . . . the beams of the hidden vault.

Suddenly, from off to the right, emerging from a hastily erected tent shelter, the black robe appeared. Matt could feel the muscles of his neck quivering. Every fiber of his body was begging him to raise and level the rifle, but the time was not yet quite ripe. He looked across the canyon again. Forget what is going on down there, he told himself. Watch for Cobre.

As he waited, Matt realized that the discovery of the ceiling beams added to his advantage. All of the Mexicans—all except the guard watching Alicia—were gathered around the hole in the ground. Probably with success so near at hand they would remain there.

Matt watched the top of the cliff across the way. Then he saw it. A momentary flash of light. Then, in a few seconds, the distant knife blade sent him another signal. In a moment he caught a fleeting glimpse of Cobre, descending through a narrow fissure in the gray rock. Then he was gone. Then nothing.

Matt waited . . . waited . . . waited. He knew that Cobre

was waiting, too. Waiting for precisely the right moment. The guard on the rock could contain his curiosity no longer. The excited men at the digging place and their shouts were too much of a temptation. The guard had to see the discovery, too. He cast aside the butt of his cigarette and slid down from the boulder . . . took a few steps. Matt slid his rifle into position.

Matt saw Cobre leap . . . arm raised with the wicked blade of the skinning knife casting off another sparkle of sunlight. The knife was in the guard's back, even before Cobre's weight knocked him to the ground. The guard never made a move. Cobre rolled off him, then sprang to his feet and leaped into the shadowed area where Alicia was being held.

Enough of that, Matt told himself. Alicia was Cobre's ward now. Matt sighted down the barrel just as one of the Mexicans yelled loudly . . . above the yells of the others' excitement. "*Intruso . . . intruso!!*" he was yelling. Bodies began milling around. Eyes followed the man's pointing finger. Matt, himself, looked across the way to the place where the guard had fallen. He saw Cobre shove Alicia up and over a large boulder. Then the Apache turned and slid the six-guns from their holsters.

Now the Mexicans were dropping their implements of work and racing madly about . . . scurrying here and there to get their weapons. A sharp pistol report tore through the morning air, and Matt saw one of the Mexicans fall. A Mexican with a rifle raced into a shallow gully and threw himself prone, facing in Cobre's direction, his back fully exposed to Matt's line of sight. Matt squeezed off a shot, and the Mexican slumped forward . . . did not move.

Cobre was firing rapidly now. Matt, too. Another Mexican fell under Matt's fusillade. The gold-digging Mexicans were in a state of total panic. Guns were firing down on them from both sides. Matt saw the black robe running . . . darting in and out among the milling bodies. Then the false priest broke into the open. Matt put him in his sights, but before he could fire, his quarry was blocked by frantic animals . . . horses pulling at their tethers . . . mules running in confused circles.

Matt looked back toward the center of the valley for an instant. He picked out a running Mexican . . . one heading toward Cobre's side of the valley with a drawn weapon. Matt missed with the first shot . . . dropped the man with his second.

He swung back toward the horses. Now he could see the black robe, swinging into a saddle. The man whipped at the horse, and it lunged forward . . . galloping through the mass of Mexicans who were trying to organize themselves into something more effective than a yelling, swirling mass of confusion.

As Matt put his cheek to his weapon, he whispered in his mind, "I know you. I've run across men like you before. The brutal bully in the body of a coward." The black-robed leader was pulling out . . . saving his own skin. And most likely, Matt told himself, already planning his next expedition into the Baboquivaris. After all, the hole was half dug by his hapless companions.

The black robe's horse was less than twenty paces from the place where the canyon jutted out. Matt held him in the sights, gently . . . ever so gently moving the barrel . . . gently, ever so gently squeezing down on the trigger. The rifle roared, and through a haze of gunsmoke Matt saw the black robe fly from the saddle and land in a heap. The galloping horse continued on and disappeared around the canyon wall.

The Mexicans below were *not* getting themselves organized. In fact, on an individual basis, they seemed to be giving up the whole idea of fighting their way out of the predicament. Maybe it had been the black robe that gave them their new direction. Most were scrambling for horses. One man *did* turn in Matt's direction and fire, but the slug glanced off a boulder five feet from Matt's shoulder. He fired back and the man turned and ran.

A group of a half dozen Mexicans had mounted up, and in a body they pounded across the valley. Two more leaped into saddles and followed. One of them wrestled a bridle on a mule . . . mounted it bareback and followed the others. Cobre continued to fire, but from his vantage point, Matt could tell it was all over. He studied the valley carefully to make sure that none of the Mexicans was lying in hiding. Cobre had also ceased firing. Silence returned to the canyon.

Matt stood up. On the far side of the canyon Cobre waved once. Matt tried to count the bodies. There were five that he could see, plus the black robe. Eight, nine . . . maybe ten had ridden out. No matter. Alicia was alive. That was really all Matt cared about.

He started back over the ridge. He would get the horses and ride down . . . meet Alicia and Cobre.

By the time Matt rode into the valley, leading Cobre's horse, the Indian was walking among the bodies . . . kicking at them to make sure they were dead. "Where's Alicia?" Matt asked as he rode up. Cobre pointed to the rocks. Matt rode toward her, and as he approached, she edged out of her hiding place.

Matt swung out of the saddle, and she lunged into his arms. He let her shake and cry for a long time. Then, with a certain suddenness, she stopped . . . looked up at him. "Matt . . . Matt . . . Matt," she said. "Thank God for Matt Ramsey."

It was a nice compliment, but Matt couldn't accept all of it. "If I hadn't run into the Indian, it wouldn't have happened."

She looked beyond Matt. Cobre was still walking among the bodies, now casually poking with the barrel of his rifle. Alicia called out. "Cobre! Thank you . . . thank you." Cobre nodded and kept at his business. Alicia looked back into Matt's face. "I've known him for two or three years. He's even eaten at the house several times, but he's never spoken a word to me."

"He *is* a man of few words," Matt replied. "I'm ready to get the hell out of these mountains. How about you?"

"Oh, Matt," she said, her voice low and full of pain. "He killed all of our men, didn't he?"

Matt nodded. "I didn't know how long we would be gone, so Juanita and Theresa are going to put them in the ground."

"Cleve is dead, too," she said, "Bob is dead." Matt put his arm around her shoulder and walked with her. Several horses, calm and feeding now that the shooting had ceased, were still in the valley. "Let me saddle you a horse."

Cobre was looking at the place where all the digging had taken place. He turned when Matt walked up. "Lots of work now. Cobre must shovel all the dirt back . . . put new plants in ground . . . drag bodies away." He picked up a shovel. "Now that Mexicans leave this, I bury the big bell . . . throw many rocks on top of it." He looked deep into Matt's eyes. "You forget this place, Ramsey. Never come back. Don't come back."

"I wouldn't dare," said Matt—and he meant it.

While Matt was saddling the horse for Alicia, a distant voice called out. All three of them turned and looked toward the far end of the valley. Someone was standing in amongst the rocks . . . waving a white handkerchief. "Señors! I am not armed. I want to come out!"

Matt dropped the saddle to the ground . . . drew and cocked his weapon. "Come on down!" he shouted. They watched curiously as the figure stepped out into the open . . . hands above his head. When he was only a few yards away, it became obvious that the surrendering Mexican was only a smooth-faced youth. Surely no more than fifteen or sixteen, Matt told himself. His eyes were the eyes of the severely frightened.

"I am not one of them," he said, speaking English with a hesitant accent. "I am only a poor horse wrangler."

"How come you were with 'em, then?" Matt asked.

"My patron, Juan Antonio Diaz, assigned me to go along . . . to care for the animals. I am not a . . . a . . . gunfighter like those others. I am not a *bandido* like Castenada."

"Castenada?" inquired Matt. "Who is that?"

"The one in the black robe. He is a very cruel man, señor. They told me all about him around the campfire . . . told me about everything. I wanted to run away, but I was afraid."

The boy had no weapons. That was obvious. Matt motioned with his pistol toward the pile of newly dug earth. "Let's sit down. I want to hear all about this."

Matt and the boy sat on the dirt. Alicia stood. Cobre squatted nearby. "What made you want to run away?" Matt asked.

"Soon after we made camp on this side of the border, I started hearing things. I was unhappy and wanted to go home, but what was I to do? Then, after they captured the *yanqui*, I knew I was among some very bad men."

Alicia stepped quickly forward. "An American? You said an American man?"

"*Sí*, señora."

"Tell me about him."

"He was a rancher, señora. That's what they told me . . . a man whose land lay in the path to the gold. That's—"

Alicia nearly leaped forward . . . knelt in the soft dirt in front of the boy. "Did he have brown hair . . . a brown mustache?"

"*Sí* señora."

Matt watched Alicia. She looked faint. But quickly she regained her composure. She took a deep breath. Matt knew what she was preparing to ask. She was preparing to ask the toughest question of her life. "Is he alive?"

"I think so, señora. He was when I saw him last."

"Where is he?"

"Mexico, señora."

Alicia looked at Matt. Matt stood up. "I'm going to go to my saddlebags and bring back some food and water. I think we need to rest a spell and let this young man tell us all he knows."

So in the bright morning sun they sat on the dirt pile and listened. "My name," said the young man, "is Bonifacio Salazar. I work as a horse wrangler for Señor Juan Antonio Diaz, on his ranch to the south of Magdalena. But I am afraid that I will have to seek employment somewhere else when I return to Mexico." The boy's face took on a very serious expression. "Señor Diaz is a man with a very black heart. I could not go back there."

Matt passed a water flask to the boy. "Is this something you just found out . . . about the man's black heart."

"*Sí*, señor. All that I tell you was learned around the campfire . . . talk between the men."

"Who were these men? Did you know them before?"

"No . . . only one of them other than myself worked on the ranch. I knew him. But I believe all the others were . . . were . . ."

Alicia tried to help. "Enlisted?"

"*Sí*. Hired by Castenada."

"Where in Mexico was my husband taken?"

"Oh, señora," said the boy in a plaintive voice, "this man was your husband?"

"Yes. Where is he?"

"They said he would be taken to the hacienda of Señor Diaz and held there."

Alicia looked up at Matt. "He's alive."

"And we'll go after him, but I want to hear it all. Bonifacio, tell us everything you know . . . from the beginning . . . just as it was told to you around the campfire."

"The whole of the story is made up of pieces . . . things that passed between these men over a period of days . . . just idle talk, I suppose, to pass the time. There was, as they told it, a renegade Jesuit priest. This priest had fallen from grace and practiced many bad and worldly habits. To do these things, he needed money. So he came to Señor Diaz and told him about some hidden gold. This priest was a historian at the mission of Caborca, and he had some very old maps and writings. He sold these to Señor Diaz."

Alicia cut in. "So that's why he sent people up here to get access to our land."

"That's correct, señora. But when he could not get the land and the clear passage into the mountains, Señor Diaz, as it was told, decided to wait and try some other plan. Then, the bad priest comes to Diaz again. He tells him that another priest, a good and kindly man named Father Arredondo, had been assigned to seek and find some old missions."

"And one of them was the mission of San Acacia del Norte," said Matt.

The boy's head nodded up and down. "So, Señor Diaz

hires the *bandido*, Castenada, and the *bandido* kills the good priest on his way north to the Estados Unidos. Then the bad Jesuit, whose name I do not know, teaches Castenada the habits and mannerisms of a priest."

Again Alicia interrupted. "That's what Juanita was talking about. He didn't really seem to know how to perform Mass and do other priestly things."

"*Sí*, señora, this Castenada was not a priest. He was known to be clever and cruel. The other men in the group were afraid of him, but, since they were bandits, too, they held him in high esteem. Then Castenada, posing as the good Father Arredondo, would go to the ranch . . . your ranch, eh? . . . and tell a lie to gain access to the mountains."

"And the rest of the men—your group—followed and waited. Right?" Matt asked.

The young Mexican nodded. Alicia asked a question. "Why did they take my husband to Mexico?"

"At first," said Bonifacio, "they were going to kill him. He had stumbled on our camp—or followed tracks there— I don't know. But Castenada said that perhaps the gringo man knew more about the Baboquivaris than he would tell. He said that maybe your husband had heard tales of the gold and knew something of its whereabouts. So . . . if the maps were not accurate and Castenada could not find the treasure they would go back to Mexico and torture the *yanqui* man."

Matt fairly leaped to his feet. "Goddammit, we can't let those who escaped get back to Mexico ahead of us. If we're going to get Cleve, we need the element of surprise!"

Alicia understood the significance of Matt's statement. She was on her feet immediately. Both turned to Cobre . . . squatting in the dirt.

"We need to leave right now, Cobre! Do you understand?"

Cobre held his hand out, palm toward Matt—a sign asking for patience and restraint. "Mexicans ride out bad way. We ride out easy way."

"We need to get ahead of them . . . beat them to Diaz's place."

Cobre rose in a leisurely fashion. "Ramsey, old friend, we not going to race with Mexicans. We are going to kill Mexicans. We don't need problem behind us and problem in front of us."

Matt understood.

Cobre turned to Alicia and spoke to her for the first time ever. "You know where three trees grow by waterhole south of hill of rocks?" Alicia said she did. "We ride there. From hill we wait and watch."

Matt turned to the young Mexican. "We need a guide."

"Señor, gladly." Bonifacio was on his feet, too. "I need to saddle a horse. And one for the señora, also."

# CHAPTER
## ★ 22 ★

By following Cobre's shorter and easier route, they came out of the Baboquivaris far south of the mountain exit that would be used by the fleeing Mexicans. They continued in a southerly direction toward the small hill of rocks which, in the distance, stood out in silhouette against the late-afternoon sky.

Just before dusk they reached the hill and, following Cobre, worked their way up the western slope to a place that provided a good view of the channel of valley that ran between the high ground and the Baboquivaris.

"How long before they get here?" Matt asked Cobre.

"Soon," was the extent of Cobre's reply to that particular question. He pointed out across the valley. "Trees and water out there. Cobre leave now. Mexican horses will want water. When they come, I shoot. When they run, Cobre will chase them this way. You shoot. Then you chase, too."

The plan sounded fine with Matt. Alicia had armed herself by taking a rifle and pistol from one of the dead Mexicans back in the canyon. Young Bonifacio had done likewise, but Matt doubted that the youth had much stomach for a gun battle. On the other hand, as Alicia's newest and only cowhand—interviewed and hired during the ride out of the mountains—he might want to prove himself to his new

158

employer. It was important, Matt told himself, that none of the gold-seekers make it back to the Diaz hacienda ahead of them. The element of surprise was critical as far as Matt was concerned.

Cobre looked to the north. Squinted into the fading light. "Mexicans come." He mounted his horse. "When they run, we follow. Ride until the last Mexican is dead."

"That's what we need to do," Matt replied.

Then Cobre was on his way. When he hit the floor of the valley, he kicked the mount into a gallop and was soon a speck racing ahead of a trail of settling dust . . . heading for the water hole.

Alicia had rolled up the sleeve of her shirt and was studying the heavily swollen lump on her forearm. "You all right?" Matt asked.

She nodded that she was. "I got a look at his eyes, just after he hit me with the barrel of his pistol. The man was purely evil, Matt."

"No more," said Matt. He turned to Bonifacio. "While we're waitin', let's put our time to good use. I want you to describe the Diaz property and the Diaz hacienda in as much detail as possible. Have you been inside the house?"

"Sí," said Bonifacio. "I had many duties while working there. I have worked in the house. Many times I have carried things in and out."

Alicia rolled down the sleeve. "Tell us everything," she said as she took a seat on the ground next to the boy.

As the sun slowly disappeared behind the peaks to the west, Bonifacio provided a detailed description of their eventual destination. Matt's interest was most intense when the youth told of the tiny room in the basement with a heavy door and small barred window. "I asked about it once, when we were stacking crates down there. This old man told me that he had once been locked in the room some years ago. In those days the frontier of Mexico was very rough. And there were no towns for a hundred kilometers or more. So in those days the room was like a jail . . . a place to put a man when he disobeyed or caused trouble. This old man said he had been very drunk on mescal and had shot his pistol off many times and killed a horse by accident. They put him in there and left him there for a long time. He didn't say how long, but he said that after that he always gave his pistol to his cousin before drinking mescal."

"Good," said Matt. "Very good."

Bonifacio went on. But at a certain point in the story, Matt reached over and touched Bonifacio's arm. "That's all for now," Matt said. "Look out there." They did. The rising dust was easy to see. Matt pointed down the hill to a place where an old saguaro stood against the sky. "You go down there, Bonifacio." He pointed to a rocky outcropping to the right. "You over there, Alicia."

Once they were positioned, there was nothing to do but wait. Now Matt could make out tiny, moving dots that were the horses. He counted them . . . nine. Closer and closer they came to the distant clump of trees that grew by the water hole.

Suddenly Matt's heart started pounding, the adrenalin pumping. He could see the line of horses suddenly break up . . . Cobre was shooting. Seconds later the dull, repetitive reports of the Indian's rifle reached the hill.

The drama of life and death moved toward them. Cobre was herding the panic-stricken Mexicans like sheep. When they tried to veer north, Cobre turned them back. When one Mexican cut his horse sharply to the right, Cobre followed . . . closed the gap . . . then raised his rifle and fired. Before the Mexican hit the ground, Cobre had turned back toward the main body. Matt counted. Six were left.

When the remnants of the fleeing band hit the base of the hill, Matt opened fire . . . Alicia followed, as did young Bonifacio. Two more dropped. Those left reined their horses sharply and raced toward the south. Matt jumped up. "Let's go." All raced for their horses.

Cobre was waiting at the bottom of the hill. He pointed in the direction that the Mexicans had taken. "No hurry. Big arroyo that way." He pointed a little to the right. "We go that way. Mexicans come back."

Cobre's prediction was precisely on target. The steep arroyo forced the Mexicans to turn, sending them back toward their pursuers. Now the whole procedure was one of chase and shoot. At one point Matt told himself that Cobre was actually playing a game with the Mexicans. They would swerve in one direction, and Cobre would cross their line of flight from the rear . . . gain on them and fire. Then, like frightened rabbits, the Mexicans would race off in the opposite direction.

After a chase of perhaps five miles, when only three were left, one decided to leave the others. Matt took off after him and dropped the man with a single shot just before he reached a thick grove of mesquites.

Night was falling fast, and Cobre, aware that the Mexicans would soon have a blanket of darkness, quit playing his game and quickly dispatched one of the last two. The final man ran his horse up a rise in the ground . . . leaped off and raced toward a cover of rocks. He started yelling in Spanish, his voice high-pitched and wavering with fright.

Cobre, in no apparent hurry, sat his horse and waited until the others joined him.

"What is he saying," Alicia asked Bonifacio.

"That is Pablo Obregon . . . the man I told you worked for Señor Diaz on the ranch. He is pleading, señora. He says he is a common workingman who has never harmed anyone. He is asking for mercy, señora."

"He's not a bandit?" asked Alicia.

"No, señora. He is much like me. He herds cattle . . . things like that."

She turned to Matt. "What do you think?"

Matt thought about it. "Are you sure, Bonifacio?"

"*Sí*. Sometimes he rides with me to the mission for Sunday Mass. He doesn't get drunk very much, and he is a good worker."

Alicia smiled a tiny smile . . . the first that Matt had seen since they rescued her in the canyon. "Ask him, Bonifacio, if he would like a job."

Bonifacio's face broke into a broad grin. He called excitedly in Spanish to the hiding Pablo. Pablo yelled back. Matt couldn't understand exactly what Pablo was saying, but his response was laced liberally with the word *gracias*.

Pablo came out of the rocks with his hands above his head and his knees shaking. "*Gracias . . . gracias . . . gracias,*" he mumbled as he drew near.

Alicia approached him, dragging Bonifacio along as interpreter. After a short exchange, Pablo accepted Alicia's offer of work. But, through Bonifacio, she cautioned her new hire. "She says that if you lie or betray her trust in any way"—Bonifacio pointed to Cobre, who stood with his rifle held across his chest—"she will send this man after you." Pablo took a quick look at Cobre and gave Bonifacio every assurance that he would be a good and trusted employee. "Then," said Bonifacio, "you must ride north to the ranch house. Approach carefully, because there has been trouble at the ranch, and the two women there might shoot you. Call from a distance and identify yourself and explain why you are there. The señora gives you something to tell them that will put their fears to rest. She says to tell the woman, Juanita, that the pattern on the best set of dishes in the house is a pattern of gold leaves and that last month she burned a roast in the oven." Bonifacio listened as Alicia conveyed some more instructions. "She says that if the woman, Juanita, still won't let you approach the house, you should camp in the valley and wait for our return."

"*Bueno, bueno,*" Pablo replied, bowing repeatedly in Alicia's direction.

Then they mounted their horses and proceeded south at a more leisurely pace. They camped that night just below the border by the banks of a small running stream. The next day was forty, dusty miles across the Sonoran Desert.

Just before nightfall the group stopped to rest briefly and finalize their plans. As they started on the last leg of the journey, Matt looked off to the southeast. He could see the flickering specks of light from windows in the community of Magdalena.

Finally Bonifacio stopped them at a certain place where a dirt road came down from plateau country off to the west. "About two or three kilometers in that direction," he told Matt.

"Good," said Matt. "We want to stay away from the place where the workers live and approach the back wall like you suggested. You go first."

They followed Bonifacio up to higher country, riding through the brush and cacti, avoiding the road. After they had traveled less than a mile, Matt could hear the distant sound of a guitar and the voice of a man singing. Then he picked up the flicker of a fire . . . then the soft glow from windows. A dog barked . . . another joined it. Bonifacio stopped. "Can you see it?" he asked, pointing. Matt could . . . with no trouble at all . . . the high walls of the hacienda of Juan Antonio Diaz.

Matt made his inquiry in a low voice. "Are we looking at the back wall?"

"*Sí.*"

Matt leaned toward Cobre. "Looks like it would be best if you went around that side . . . stay away from the huts over there." Cobre nodded. Matt turned to Bonifacio. Bonifacio had told Matt and Alicia earlier that Diaz employed a small group of gunslingers to enforce discipline on the ranch and serve as a fighting nucleus in case of Indian attack. "No more than maybe five or six," Bonifacio had said. One man, Bonifacio said, was always on duty at night, guarding the main-gate entry to the hacienda.

"I go now," Cobre said, and he slipped off his mount and melted in the darkness.

"Take us to the back gate," Matt said and Bonifacio led the way. There was a convenient hitching rail near the solid door entrance. The boy and Alicia dismounted and tied their horses. Tied Cobre's also. Matt remained in the saddle. In a matter of only minutes Cobre was back. Matt knew without asking that Cobre's knife had taken care of the guard.

Matt spoke softly to Bonifacio. "I want you to stay here with the horses. Are you sure no one will come up and cause a problem?"

"No, señor. These people work hard all day. Very soon they will go to sleep. I know all the people. If someone does come, they won't bother me."

Bonifacio had told Matt that the back gate—like the front one—was barred and bolted from the inside. They approached it cautiously, even though Bonifacio assured Matt that it was unguarded. The wall was twelve feet high. Cobre leaned his rifle against it, just to the side of the gate. Then he removed his gunbelt and handed it to Alicia.

Matt positioned his buckskin against the wall, then removed a boot from the stirrup. Cobre put his foot into the empty stirrup and pulled himself up behind Matt. Then he stood up, braced against the wall, and climbed to Matt's shoulders . . . hoisted himself to the top of the wall and disappeared over it.

Matt trotted his mount back to the hitching rail, dismounted, and returned to the wall. He and Alicia waited. Very soon the door swung open. They entered silently and proceeded toward the massive two-story house.

Bonifacio had suggested an entry on the south side of the place, near the back. The three of them stepped softly to a covered tile porch that ran the length of the building . . . then moved through deep shadows to the door. Matt looked in through a window. A woman was putting dishes away.

Bonifacio had described the Diaz cook. The woman putting the dishes away fitted the description. Her name, Bonifacio had said, was Maria. Alicia edged to the door . . . Matt continued to watch through the window. Alicia tapped on the door. Maria called out, *"Qué?"* But she continued to stack plates and saucers.

Alicia looked toward Matt. With his hand he signaled for her to knock again. She did. Again Maria called out. *"Qué?"*

This time Alicia called softly. "Maria."

The woman slid some plates into the cupboard and crossed the room. Cobre was standing at the door . . . back to the wall. When it opened, he jerked the plump woman onto the porch and placed his hand across her mouth with enough force to make her eyes bug out. Cobre, like many Apache who raided and intermittently lived in Mexico, could speak Spanish.

He told Maria that they meant her no harm . . . at least she would not be harmed if she remained quiet. Then he asked where Señor Diaz was at that very moment and who else was in the house.

Cobre turned to Matt. "All are in the dining room. Diaz, three other men, one woman."

"Ask her if there is a man being held in the basement room."

The woman's eyes grew saucer-shaped with fright when Cobre posed the question. In Spanish she told Cobre that there was a man there, and that she took him good food—even fruit twice a day—that she also took him soap and water to wash with . . . that she treated him in a kindly manner . . . Cobre put his hand back across her mouth and spared Matt the details. "He's there."

Matt replied. "Tell her that we are going to release her and she should go out the back gate quietly. If she disobeys, she will be severely punished."

Cobre translated liberally. He told her that he would slice her throat if she made a sound. Then he let her go. They watched as Maria waddled across the yard at a fast but ungainly pace.

Then they entered. Cobre first, because he spoke Spanish. They crossed the kitchen . . . paused only a moment. Matt nodded his head. Cobre threw the door open. *"Manos arriba! Manos arriba!"* he shouted.

The five people at the table did exactly as ordered. The one at the head of the table was obviously Diaz . . . a relatively distinguished-looking man with gray hair. But there was something hard and ruthless in his eyes. Diaz glared at them. One of his hands remained below the tabletop. *"Arriba,"* growled Cobre. Diaz obeyed, but the muscles along his jaw twitched with anger.

Matt scanned the table. The other three were younger men. The woman was young, also . . . with heavy makeup and a hard look about her. Maria had said that there were no others in the house. Matt spoke to Cobre. "Tell them that if anyone makes one funny move, I will blow him to hell."

Cobre relayed the message. "Now," said Matt, "tell them all to stand up." The group stood. The hired men wore guns. "Guns on the table," Matt said. Cobre passed the message, and the gunbelts went on the table. "All right, Cobre, you take Alicia downstairs and release Cleve."

The pendulum of a large standing clock swung back and forth. There was a pronounced silence in the room. The man farthest from Diaz said something in Spanish. The man nearest Diaz answered. "No talk," said Matt.

In a few moments the talk started again. This time Matt extended the barrel of his weapon in the direction of the man speaking. The talk stopped.

The man nearest Diaz lifted his hand from the table and casually slid it inside his jacket . . . scratched at his stomach. Matt fixed his eyes on the man . . . took a step in his direction. In a fleeting fraction of a second, as his peripheral vision picked up sudden movement, Matt realized that the scratching was a ruse. His real problem was the man farthest away. Matt whirled as the small pistol, pulled from a boot, was leveled in his direction. Matt and the armed Mexican fired in the same instant. As the Mexican reeled back, hit in the chest, Matt felt a harsh stinging sensation on the outside of his left thigh, then shocking pain that collapsed the leg and sent him to the floor.

He heard the clatter on top of the table . . . guns being fumbled for. Matt could see only legs. He aimed and fired, and another of Diaz's gunslingers crumpled with a bullet through his knee. When the man hit the floor, Matt saw that he had a pistol in his hand. Matt fired again, and the Mexican collapsed in a motionless heap. Another set of legs moved toward the end of the table. The man fired through the tabletop, but the wood-splintering shot missed Matt by three feet. Matt pulled the trigger as he rolled away. The man went down, and Matt finished him with a second shot.

One shot left. Matt slithered under the table. No longer were there legs in sight. But he could hear the sound of running feet. He emerged from under the table. The hard-faced woman was running up the stairs. He ignored her. It was

Diaz he wanted. He shoved himself to his feet . . . lurched through a wide doorway . . . saw Diaz as he threw open the front door. Matt fired once. Missed.

The leg was burning as though it had been chewed on by a thousand red ants. For a moment Matt thought he might faint. He leaned against a wall . . . removed his kerchief from his neck. There were bottles of tequila and whiskey on the table. Matt limped back in the dining room . . . sloshed some tequila into the shallow wound, then wrapped the cloth around it. Then he reloaded his weapon.

Noise . . . feet pounding up wooden stairs. Matt listened carefully. He couldn't tell for sure if it was two sets of footsteps or three. Then they burst into the room. Cleve wore a stunned, incredulous look. It intensified when he saw Matt. "Sonofabitch," he muttered.

Matt was hurting, but the hurt was wiped out by the sudden appearance of his friend. "I thought you invited me down here for a rest," Matt replied. But then it was back to business. "Diaz went out the front door."

Matt went first, limping . . . Cobre at his shoulder . . . Alicia and Cleve behind. In the darkness of the long porch they stood quietly. "Front gate is still closed," Matt whispered.

"Shh," Cobre replied. The Indian slipped across the porch, stood very quietly . . . peering into the darkness. He motioned with his arm. The others joined him where he stood behind a thick adobe pillar. "He is at the far corner of the yard, pressed into the dark corner where the two high walls come together."

"I can't see him," said Matt.

"Does he have a weapon?" Alicia asked.

"Maybe," replied Cobre. "He holds something."

"Step back," Alicia said as she worked her way to the corner of the pillar. "I'm going to take care of this." Then she called out in a loud voice. "You are responsible for killing four of my men, Diaz. Walk toward me with your arms in the air."

The only reply was silence.

"Cobre," Alicia inquired, "is he still there?"

"Yes."

She shouted again. "Pete Waggoner was my foreman! Bob Whipple, José Escobar, and Manuel Garza were my cowboys. You killed them, Diaz!" Then in a lower voice to Cobre, "Is he still there?"

"Yes."

"Right where the walls come together?"

"Yes."

She cocked the rifle, raised it, and took aim. "Is he standing up?"

"Yes."

The harsh report of the rifle broke the stillness of the night. She worked the lever . . . threw another round into the chamber. Turned to Cobre. "Is he still standing?"

"No, señora, the man is no longer standing."

They rode through the night, seeking the border. A slice of moon hung in the sky to the north. Cleve and Alicia had taken the lead, riding side by side . . . held in silhouette by the soft moonlight. Bonifacio was next. Cobre and Matt brought up the rear. Matt looked up. A countless scatter of stars filled the sky from horizon to horizon.

Matt turned to Cobre. "You going back to the mountains?"

"Yes," said Cobre.

"Doesn't it get lonely up there?"

"Sometimes," said Cobre, "but I don't mind. That is my nature. I have work to do when I get back. Bury the big bell and change the land. Make it like it was."

"Have you ever heard of Texas?"

"Yes . . . a place far away."

"There's a lot of Mexican people in Texas. They have dark skin . . . many look a great deal like you. You speak English . . . speak Spanish. You would not be a hunted man in Texas. We could give you a new name. You could get a job."

"Where?"

"Maybe Laredo . . . maybe San Angelo."

"What are those places? Are they like agency?"

"Much bigger than an agency. They're cities."

For the first time Cobre laughed. It was a deep, full laugh that carried on the night air. "You mean white-eyes running all over like ants." This time the laugh boomed out across the desert. "You must be loco, Ramsey!"